I0831910

THE WINDOW

THE WINDOW

A NOVEL

Anto Krajina

IDEOS

This novel and all characters in it are fictitious. Any resemblance to real events or persons, living or dead, is purely coincidental.

Published by Ideos Publications Ltd. in Zürich, London and Hong Kong.

For general information on our other products please visit www.ideospublications.com

All books by Ideos Publications are also available as eBooks.

Cover: Anto Krajina and David Kobelt Grafikdesign, Switzerland.

Printed in the United Kingdom.

CIP Catalogue record for this book is available from the British Library.

ISBN 978-3-9523859-4-4

THE WINDOW

THE WINDOW

It was early in the morning and the roofs of Clermont were still wrapped in darkness. Not a step could be heard either in the wide main street or in the tiny, winding side lanes. That was quite unusual for a thriving, dynamic little town where even during the small hours at least some drunks would loiter on unsteady feet. The town's pigeons themselves were not cooing, as if they too knew that all the people were still asleep.

The autumn season had just begun, the time immediately after the harvest, when everyone is striving to gather and shelter the fruits of their efforts. The granaries were filled up with new grain, the barns were spreading a pleasant smell of fresh hay and healthy livestock were resting in the stables.

The grapes were exceptionally sweet and juicy and exceeded the wine-growers' wildest expectations. All of them were convinced that the wine, the fermentation of which had just begun, would be of excellent quality and each of them thought of keeping back a certain quantity of the liquid bliss for the coming years as something precious, each sip of which might be a temptation to praise former times as better and happier and to forget – at least for a short while – all their troubles.

The most strenuous and most important period of the year had been successfully completed. The night before the harvest was crowned with a festival. Even the most modest of families allowed themselves a sumptuous meal and the pleasant odour of the freshly pressed grape juice filled their sitting-rooms.

All the people were exhausted and satisfied and allowed themselves a long sleep the morning after. Each one was dreaming, in accordance with his wishes, apprehensions, inclinations and capabilities, his own dream.

*

In that respect Rue des Gras was no different. That morning the only conspicuous thing about the tiny, sleepy lane, one of the quietest and most pleasant streets of Clermont, was the dim candle light in a window of one of the houses.

It was the house in which Etienne Pascal, his three children, their aunt Marie and Louise, the servant, lived. Etienne Pascal was a respectable government official and held the office of the Head of the Revenue Office of Clermont. His office required a solid knowledge of mathematics, diligence, punctuality as well as unconditional loyalty to the State and the Crown. Etienne Pascal was an exemplary official in whose person all these qualities were most happily combined. He enjoyed the unlimited confidence of the Chancellor of the Exchequer and his counsel was welcome even in the highest circles of the state apparatus. Being an excellent mathematician he had close contacts among some of the leading scientists in the kingdom, which was regarded by many as the most beautiful one in the entire world. One could, of course, have argued about whether they were right or not as about many other things, however it couldn't be denied that people who lived there were deeply convinced that their native land was the most beautiful of all.

Etienne Pascal's prestigious position provided great advantages and promised a pleasant future for his children. Each of his three children was gifted in a certain way; however, their talents and interests were completely different.

Gilberte, his elder daughter, didn't read any books, nor was she a friend of logical thinking and she abhorred mathematics. She was only ten when she zealously helped Louise, the faithful servant, in the tiny garden behind the house, in the kitchen and in the washing-room; she washed and ironed, sewed and knitted indefatigably. When it came to abstract things she was Etienne Pascal's least talented child and at the same time the most beloved one by all people who knew him and his children.

Jacqueline, the younger daughter, read indefatigably the works of the great authors and even herself wrote touching verses and charming diaries. She didn't have any talent for mathematics or logic either. Reading religious books, in particular those dealing with the lives of the saints, offered her the greatest pleasure.

Etienne Pascal was especially proud of his second child, his only son Blasius, because he believed that his son had the same characteristics as he himself – sharp logical thinking and exemplary persistence when it came to getting to the bottom of something.

Etienne Pascal loved them all and lived for them.

*

Antoinette Pascal, née Begon, Etienne Pascal's wife, had died several years before. The acuteness of mind, a striking feature in Etienne Pascal and his son, was in the late Antoinette Pascal even more pronounced. She died before Blasius was three years old. None of the three children could remember her. They knew her only from what their father had told them about her. He used the words "angel on earth" when he spoke of her. That was the reason that the children, who loved and admired their father above all, thought of their mother as an angel in the way naïve people think of angels: holy, immaculate, otherworldly, celestial. And they were aware of being the children of such an angelic, ideal mother.

Their father was for them the embodiment of honesty, correctness and goodness. The result of his complete devotion and sacrifice was that his children didn't notice the early loss of their mother at all, or they at least weren't aware of the fact that they were lacking motherly love. A sort of blessing in disguise was the fact that immediately after Antoinette Begon's death, her sister began looking so devotedly after the little orphans that their mother wouldn't have been able to do it better.

Thus life in Etienne Pascal's home was filled with peace and satisfaction. Nothing happened that might have disturbed the harmony. The children thrived and learnt – in accordance with their capabilities – under their father's loving protection.

Etienne Pascal regularly participated in meetings of personalities in Clermont who were interested in mathematics and sciences and thereby he kept himself currently informed of the latest achievements of the intellectual elite of the whole country.

Thus in the life of Etienne Pascal and his children things couldn't be better. And yet something happened that early morning that induced him to abandon the idyll of a peaceful provincial town and move with his children to that town in which all the strings of the entire Kingdom converged.

*

Etienne Pascal was an early riser although he used to go to bed quite late, because he needed little sleep, which is often the case in people with higher mental capacity.

That morning, he got up even earlier than usual, because he wanted to finish some work before leaving for Paris. In the Ministry of Finance he was to have very important talks and he wasn't sure if he would have enough time later to meet his engagements in his own office in Clermont. He had been informed by the Minister himself that an extensive tax reform was near. However, it was not yet known what the reform would be like and when it would come into effect. Being one of the most capable and most important revenue officers in the country, he was invited to Paris for consultations on that matter. The invitation was signed by the Minister himself, which suggested that the matter was of particular importance.

After he had got up and taken a bath Etienne Pascal went to his children's bedrooms. Since the death of his wife that was how he started almost each of his days.

Both girls were sleeping peacefully in their rooms and didn't hear that someone had opened the door. He did it very gently so that only someone who wasn't asleep might have heard it.

He opened the door of Blasius' room in the same manner; however, there he had a surprise that went beyond his fondest dreams. His son was just seven years old and at that tender age he already exhibited a unique scientific curiosity as well as the adequate intellectual capacity to satisfy that curiosity, which in the entire human history happened only very rarely.

Etienne Pascal was acquainted with the fact that Blasius had always wanted to know special and unexpected things and that therefore his questions also had a particular character. However, what he found that morning surpassed all he had known before and he decided that same day to look for a suitable house in Paris during his short stay there with the intention to take up permanent residence in the capital.

When he opened the door a candle was burning in Blasius' room. The boy was sitting at his desk and reading a book usually used by mathematicians and students of mathematics with the intention of filling certain gaps in their knowledge of geometry. It was the book by that famous Greek mathematician who many centuries ago managed to collect and exhaustively comment on all that was known in the field of geometry at that time. Due to its exemplary punctuality and exhaustiveness the work had survived and served as the best textbook for numerous generations of mathematicians over centuries. The beauty and the greatness of that work of genius was the fact that it could – being completely independent of place and time – serve all practical purposes satisfactorily. The cases for which it wouldn't be sufficient aren't known in practical life.

Etienne Pascal stood, still holding onto the handle, in the half-opened door for a few seconds and could neither speak nor stir.

Blasius was sitting at his desk and his little childlike face was glowing in the soft, golden candlelight. Only the large book leaning against the rest, the boy's face and the tiny hands were lit while all the else in the room seemed to be plunged in complete darkness.

The boy - obviously very surprised at his father's unexpected visit – didn't stir.

The instant crystallized into a consummate picture.

The boy hadn't done anything wrong though, and yet his feeling was close to a sense of guilt. He had done something secretly at a time when he was supposed to be asleep. His behaviour created in his father the impression that in his home something happened without his knowledge and it was something that he should have known.

A timid "Father!" broke the silence. It sounded like an attempt to make sure his father was not cross with him, for he had done something without permission, although it wasn't expressly forbidden. In the way the boy uttered "Father!" and in his face, there was a note of "Are you angry with me?" as well as "Please don't be angry with me", a question and a plea at the same time.

Etienne Pascal was speechless, because what he saw was so overwhelming that he couldn't find a suitable word to express what he was feeling in that moment. He approached the boy gently smiling, stroked his head and looked him in the face without saying anything. For an instant he had the impression that his beloved Antoinette was standing in front of him. He kissed the boy on his forehead and asked him why he had got up so early. The parallels didn't allow him to sleep any longer, answered the boy in his fine child's voice. To his father's question what he meant by that he answered that the parallels had tempted him irresistibly to wander between them further and further by promising to merge in the distance, however, they remained stubbornly separate. Etienne Pascal asked the boy what his opinion about the parallels was.

"They can meet only over there, never here," answered Blasius.

Etienne Pascal felt that the words of his little son bore a tremendous message, however he didn't want to ask him any further questions about that. He sat down beside the boy and asked him what he was reading.

"The *Elements* by Euclid," answered Blasius.

And how far had he come, asked Etienne Pascal. The boy answered that he had already read and understood everything and that he could explain any segment of it, however, he couldn't understand one thing.

"Which one?" asked Etienne Pascal, curious and not quite without anxiety.

The boy looked at him with his big eyes, which – because of the boy's pointed chin – seemed to be far apart, and said in a hardly audible voice: "The infinite".

For a second they kept silent, because the vibrations of "the infinite" filled the air and didn't permit any conversation on it.

The boy was pale and his skin was like new parchment.

Etienne Pascal stood up. "Now I have to do some very important things and you should go and get a little more sleep – later we'll have an exhaustive conversation on everything".

"Yes, father, I'll go and have some more sleep," said the boy and the way he said it revealed how happy he was. He stood up and went to his bed. His long white nightshirt reached down almost to the floor, making his feet invisible and creating the impression that he was gliding forward without walking. Etienne Pascal put out the candle on the desk; the darkness swallowed the angelic picture. "Sleep well, my son," he added and shut the door softly behind himself.

Lost in thought, he went to his study where a pile of all sorts of letters was waiting for him, sheets of paper full of strange signs that had a special meaning and were to be taken seriously, because they were invented by man and used in a regulated system in which everything had its own fixed place.

At his desk, he halted for a second. He glanced at the sheet that was lying on top and his eyes got caught in the maze of the neatly written letters and numbers.

"They are the freest children of the intellect and the fantasy, the most noble of all parents, harnessed to a carriage of purposes," he thought and sat down in the comfortable armchair upholstered in greenish leather.

***

It was early in the morning and all the people in the house in which Etienne Pascal had his new residence since he had moved from Clermont to Paris were still asleep.

Only Louise, who had been employed as a servant with Etienne Pascal for years, was already up.

When Antoinette Pascal was expecting her first child she felt very weak, which forced the young couple to look for a maid to help out. They found in Louise someone who they later didn't want to do without. She remained with Etienne Pascal and witnessed all that happened in the family, the birth of all three children, and the unstoppable, premature perishing of his dainty, gentle and exceptionally intelligent wife. She also attended her up to the last second. Shortly before she deceased, Antoinette Pascal gave Louise a ring that she – while still the maiden Antoinette Begon – used to wear.

All that created strong ties between the family Pascal and the servant, who though lacking even basic education, was endowed with a remarkable natural intelligence, so that she had never considered leaving Etienne Pascal's home.

After Antoinette's death, her sister Marie regarded it as the highest meaning and purpose in her life to look after her sister's little orphans with such loving devotion that they didn't miss motherly love, and yet Etienne Pascal never thought of doing without Louise's devotion and trustworthiness.

*

That morning, Louise was up as usual before daybreak and busy with clearing up quietly so that everything would be in order when Aunt Marie and the two girls got up.

Etienne Pascal and Blasius weren't at home. They had gone to Rouen and intended to be back before lunch.

She had already cleared up in the kitchen, in the dining-room, in Etienne Pascal's study and was now in Blasius' room, the last room that she wanted to clean. There was, in fact, hardly anything to be cleaned, because she cleaned his room daily and Blasius for his part was an exceptionally orderly boy. Thus there wasn't much to do in his room.

Just as she started to wipe the already impeccably clean desk she caught sight of a rather large sheet of paper with various drawings on it. She halted for a second and looked at the strange lines closely, although she couldn't, of course, make any sense of them or relate them to anything. Some of the lines were straight, some were curves, some were circles, some stretched circles and all intersected. Louise knew that Blasius was considered by everybody in the house as an extremely intelligent creature, because he could calculate anything in a matter of seconds without writing it down. When asked how he could do that he answered that he could see everything already calculated and didn't have to make any effort, because everything was so easy. Although Etienne Pascal himself was an excellent mathematician he was also amazed at his son's exceptional ability to deal with numbers. He considered him to be a special case, in particular since the experience in Blasius' room, which had induced him to move to Paris.

Four years had passed since that day, Blasius was now eleven years old and all the people under Etienne Pascal's roof felt at home in Paris. Etienne Pascal had a lot of things to do, for apart from having his obligations in Paris he was still in charge of the Revenue Office in Clermont. It should be added that he was a man in the so-called prime of his life and didn't want to give up the pleasures of socializing with other people completely. It was even more astonishing therefore that he, in spite of all his obligations, managed to find enough time for his children to be their main teacher and educator.

He himself frequented the salon of Madame Sainctot, a particularly attractive lady, where many learned men gathered to exchange ideas and opinions, or simply because they secretly cherished the hope of perhaps sometime winning her favours. Whether, in this respect, Etienne Pascal was in a privileged position can't be found out, for the only thing generally known was that they highly honoured each other. It seems that Madame Sainctot always had time for Etienne Pascal and that the first question she always asked her most faithful and most regular visitors, Desargues and Roberval, was if Etienne Pascal was also coming.

In Madame Sainctot's salon he also met Mr Le Pailleur, a talented mathematician who introduced him to the most learned circles of Paris society. He soon became a member of Père Mersenne's Academy. As he himself was interested in sciences he enjoyed associating with intelligent and educated people, however, he did it primarily to pave the way of success for his son.

*

While Louise was contemplating the strange drawing she didn't notice that she was soliloquizing all the time. Aunt Marie's voice from the adjacent room shook her out of her thoughts. Aunt Marie had already got up and as she had heard Louise's voice she asked her who she was speaking to.

"To nobody, Madam," answered Louise and said that she was alone in the room. Aunt Marie could make sure of this and see it for herself when she entered the room. Louise was standing beside the desk and gazing in wonder at the innumerable lines that were intersecting or – depending on the point of view – converging or diverging.

"But you spoke to someone," insisted Aunt Marie, "I heard it."

"Not that I know of, Madam, I was just marvelling at these drawings," she said, pointing to the maze of lines on the large sheet of paper.

"I know all letters, Madam, capital letters and small ones, because I have learnt all of them, but never before have I seen letters like these that Blasius has put in the corners."

"Oh, dear Louise, don't rack your brains over such things," said Aunt Marie, and in the way she said it one could also hear an undertone, the intention which was to dissuade the curious servant from doing anything that might have given her the idea of thinking that she wasn't stupid, that she could also learn what was reserved exclusively for those who were wealthy and therefore considered to be better and cleverer than others.

"You are probably right, Madam, I don't know what these lines mean, but there's something in them that I feel attracted to, however I couldn't explain what it is."

Aunt Marie didn't like the servant's words at all, because they obviously meant that a servant could also be endowed with the ability to be attracted to higher things.

Therefore she proceeded in order to prevent the feeling created in the servant's mind from condensing and taking the shape of a thought, because a thought could very easily become a midwife of a particular stance and way of living.

"I believe you, dear Louise," she said with almost exaggerated friendliness, "everyone should, however, know their place and be careful in order not to run into a domain which is not appropriate for them."

Louise didn't say anything and for a short while the two women were standing there silently beside each other. Louise had the impression that Aunt Marie, despite her friendliness, wanted to say something different, the purpose of which was to discourage the servant from thinking about certain things and scrutinizing something that lies beyond the scope of the life of a servant. The silence was charged and depressing. Aunt Marie had noticed that the servant had some notion of what she was up to. Therefore she proceeded in order to dispel the servant's potential doubts about the honesty and sincerity of her words.

"I can't understand," she said in a reasonable, matter-of-fact way, "why Blasius leaves his papers like that, for what is written on them gives rise to confusion and stupid ideas in small people like us. But wait a second! I'll put the sheets in the drawer so that we can work undisturbed."

No sooner had she said that than she was about to carry out her intention, but Louise was faster.

"No, Madam!" she said loudly, almost shouting.

"And why not?" asked Aunt Marie, startled.

"Blasius has expressly ordered that nobody is authorised to touch his sheets," answered Louise self-confidently, because in that moment she felt to be in a sense the confidante of someone whose word and will were higher than Aunt Marie's decisions.

Aunt Marie had to give way. She knew that Blasius' wish had to be respected and – pretending to be unconcerned with the matter – said: "Well, if that is the case, he'll know better." She felt defeated, almost humiliated, because the party represented by her servant had won. In order to cover that, she added: "I just wanted to tell you, dear Louise, that everyone is attracted to something like a fly, and that each irresistible attraction contains a refuge and a grave at the same time."

Aunt Marie was in the habit of occasionally quoting sentences containing all sorts of maxims which she had learnt by heart. She hardly understood their meaning, however, they sounded good and because of their general character they were never completely rejected by the interlocutor.

Louise didn't understand completely the sense of Aunt Marie's words, but they sounded good and were impressive, for they joined refuge and death – at first sight two completely different things – into one whole and all that was the consequence of human curiosity and of being interested in things.

She remained silent for a second and then remarked: "What you have just said, Madam, is too high for me, however, I have the feeling that I have a vague idea of what you wanted to say."

Aunt Marie looked at her without saying anything, because she had the impression that the servant could comment on her words, while she herself could hardly add anything.

"What shows the way leads up to the very end and contains the end itself," said Louise, without waiting for Aunt Marie's answer.

Aunt Marie didn't understand her servant's words, but she had the impression that Louise's way of speaking was somewhat strange and not at all proper for common servants. A feeling of inferiority crept upon her, because suddenly her servant seemed to be more intelligent than herself and she felt that she had to say something. She began pretending to be calm and superior, because the servant had to be prevented by any means from thinking that she personally was not necessarily less intelligent than her landlady.

"Be happy, dear Louise, that you can only sense, because sensibility suffices for small people completely, it has a permanent value as it were, because it remains sensibility for ever. Understanding or knowledge, however, is never what it seems to be but something completely different, it has no lasting value." She spoke surely and fluently without being aware how she could utter such a sentence at all. She sensed though that what she said sounded somehow good, however, she didn't understand what she said. Once, Etienne Pascal expressed himself in that way in a conversation. She had listened to him carefully and, because she knew that he was very intelligent, she memorized his words with the intention to use them occasionally, without trying to understand them. As she knew that his words made sense she thought that anything that made sense could be said any time; the listener should try to find the point of contact; if he didn't manage to do that, then he himself was to be blamed.

Aunt Marie liked very much what Etienne Pascal had said during the conversation that time. She had repeated it again and again until she could say it fluently. Louise liked very much what Aunt Marie had said about sensibility and all of a sudden she had the impression that the two of them belonged together. She asked Aunt Marie whether Blasius wasn't too young, after all, for dealing with such tasks, because she knew that most children at his age were still playing with each other light-heartedly and that hardly any of them was interested in the maze of the strange lines. She thought that such complicated drawings were used only by highly educated adults who were building houses and bridges, or by land surveyors. She knew that Blasius had nothing to do with such things and therefore couldn't understand what he needed such drawings for.

"On the one hand he is too young for practically everything; on the other hand he is far ahead of almost all adults and understands whatever they say; they, however, don't understand what he says."

Suddenly, Jacqueline, Etienne Pascal's youngest child, butted in on their conversation. She had been in her room, had half heard what Aunt Marie and Louise were talking about and had come to join them in the conversation. In fact, she wouldn't have come at all, however the saint's history she had just read was nothing special, because it was lacking the precious turning point – the Saint didn't become a saint after an unexpected conversion by God's grace but was a pious person from the very beginning. The life stories she liked most were those of Apostle Paul and Saint Augustine, because before their conversion each one of them was in his particular way a big sinner.

"May I know what you've been chatting so nicely about?" she asked.

Aunt Marie pointed to the drawings on the desk.

"Just look at it. Who could make head or tail of all these lines, circles, semicircles, stretched circles and goodness knows what else?"

"I know what all that is about," said Jacqueline with some pride in her contribution to the conversation.

"Well, tell us then," insisted Aunt Marie with curiosity.

"Recently, Blasius saw some works by Monsieur Desargues and found them interesting. Now he wants to comment and to amplify them," said Jacqueline with a touch of triumph.

"That's quite interesting," said Aunt Marie, "and I am sure it must be something very important, for he has been working on it for some days now. By the way, how do you know that?"

"Blasius has told me everything. It is about very important things in connection with ..."

She put her right hand on her forehead, thinking and trying to find the right word, however in vain.

"I can't remember anymore what the stuff is called," she said then, "my memory fails me. I just know that it is a strange body that has the same form as the pointed hats that the young women in Bourgogne used to wear two hundred years ago. At the one end it is round and wide and towards the other end it tapers off to a fine point. I don't understand what he needs something like that for. Nor do I understand why someone can bother with such things for such a long time. But I know one thing for sure: I find such a hat ugly and I would never wear it."

"You shouldn't speak like that," Aunt Marie interrupted her, "when he deals with it for such a long time, then it must be something very special. I like calculating, however, I can't understand these drawings at all. My late sister, your mother, my sweetheart," she said while stroking Jacqueline's head, "was like Blasius, I think he got it from her."

"Not from our father?" Jacqueline asked, full of curiosity.

"He has, of course, inherited mathematical talent from his father as well, there is no doubt about that, however sons get more from their mother than from their father."

"And daughters?" Jacqueline went on asking.

"They get an equal part from either parent."

"Where did you get that from, Auntie?"

"I got it from my father and he got it from a shepherd."

"Does this here have to do anything with calculating?" asked Jacqueline, pointing to Blasius' drawings.

"I think so, it is called geometry, but it belongs to mathematics."

"I love poetry, but I don't care that much for mathematics," said Jacqueline with a smile, while pushing the nail of her right thumb under the nail of her right middle finger and producing an audible short, snapping sound.

Aunt Marie gave a short laugh.

"Auntie, do you know what ...," asked Jacqueline, trying to find the word, "oh yes, geometry is about?"

Aunt Marie felt important and superior again, for while she was talking to Jacqueline, Louise was listening to them without saying a word. She didn't make any remark nor did she ask any questions, because she was afraid Aunt Marie would find a pretext for sending her away.

She could easily understand all she heard, and yet it impressed her, for it was completely new to her. Therefore she wished to stay and hear more.

"Ahem, what geometry is about," proceeded Aunt Marie and smiled with an air of importance and satisfaction. « Blasius told me recently what it is all about. Sometimes

I think I understand what he has said to me, sometimes, however, I feel I don't. If I am honest, the latter corresponds rather to the real state of my understanding."

Louise liked Aunt Marie's words very much; they gave her courage, for they proved that other people did not understand everything all the time either, despite having enjoyed private tuition for many years.

"Do you remember what he said to you?" Jacqueline asked Aunt Marie.

"I believe that I still remember it properly. I think he has said that geometry deals with the fictive world based only on pure intellect".

"Exactly!" shouted Jacqueline, as if she had found her dearest ring, which she had thought missing. "You have already told me that several times, but I keep forgetting it."

"Oh, dear Jacquie, don't be surprised, thoughts of this kind can be easier forgotten than remembered."

"And what was that other bit about the world and the intellect? You told me that one more than once, too, didn't you?"

"I believe I know what you mean. You probably have in mind what he once told me while we were going to Mass," said Aunt Marie just to make sure that she meant the same thing.

"Exactly!" screamed Jacqueline. "What was it again?"

Aunt Marie closed her eyes to rid her mind of any other thought except the one she wanted to voice loudly and clearly, and with utter aplomb she said: "The intellect wants to force the world to be to its liking, and the world forces the intellect to be the way it is."

"Exactly! Exactly!" shouted Jacqueline repeatedly while hitting her palms against each other and bouncing up and down on both legs.

"Oh my!" she shouted. "That sounds so strange. Let me try to repeat it: The intellect ... no, the world forces ... no, the intellect forces ..."

While she was struggling to say it, she hit the writing desk with her hand with each attempt, as if trying to separate single meaningful units from one another; however none of them made any sense.

"Oh no, Auntie, this is either senseless or I don't understand it."

"I cannot tell you, dear Jacquie, with certainty which is true, but it surely can't be senseless. He never says senseless things; what he says is simply peculiar and incomprehensible for many."

"Do you understand it, Auntie?" asked Jacqueline, and her expression showed at the same time the absence of that sharpness of mind which was clearly recognizable on her brother's face, and the presence of that specific sadness which is apparent on the faces of people whose intellectual ability reaches just far enough for them to be aware of their own limitations.

"I would not like to maintain that," replied Aunt Marie, "but I feel that his words contain something essential. I tend to think about them before going to bed. I repeat them again and again before I fall asleep. This has become a habit, almost a kind of addiction, which chases away all other thoughts and concerns."

"But can you still fall asleep then, because after such thoughts you must have a headache?"

"I can fall asleep, because my brain becomes tired, but then I dream about it every time. These words accompany me even in my sleep, when I have no desires and no clear feelings. There, they appear unfailingly and wait for me. They cause peculiar laws to arise in the land of no laws and no order."

"So what are your dreams, Auntie?"

"I have the same dream all the time: I fall down a waterfall. But instead of moving downwards I move upwards."

"But, really, this is a mad dream – I would like to dream such a thing myself. You must dictate those words to me; I will write them down and repeat them until I can recite them perfectly. I will do anything to have such a dream."

Jacqueline spoke with full determination which contained a breath of desire; her eyes shone, and her expression seemed strange to Aunt Marie.

"Try to think about these words before you go to bed," said Aunt Marie, "and maybe you'll be lucky enough to give birth to the mad dream. The more you think about it, the better the chance of succeeding will be."

"Oh really, then I will think about it all the time, and then the dream will come, right, dearest Auntie? Promise me that it will come, please!" Jacqueline urged Aunt Marie, as if she had been responsible for the erratic appearance of the dream.

"Do not forget, dear child, that a dream can't be ordered or coerced. One can create the conditions for it to come, but it still doesn't depend on one's wishes and desires. Actually the opposite seems to be the case: if one tries hard to make it come, it fails to do so. And sometimes it comes even as an uninvited guest, like a thief in the night – that is its nature."

While Aunt Marie and Jacqueline spoke to each other, Louise was quiet and pretended to dust the small objects on Blasius' writing desk.

Jacqueline pricked up her ears.

"Oh, I heard something, somebody opened the front door," she said and ran downstairs. Aunt Marie followed her.

Louise was busy cleaning the corner behind Blasius' bed and pretended not to have noticed Jacqueline and Aunt Marie leave.

Now she was alone in the room and could look at the strange drawings on the writing desk undisturbed.

"Oh," she said with a quiet sigh, "I wish I could understand what these lines signify. From what Aunt Marie has said I have probably understood nothing, but nevertheless I drew great pleasure from it. I like all that about the world and the intellect best. I find it amusing that the intellect and the world influence, even force each other to be what they are. Therefore the mind as a part of the whole world contains the whole world, and the whole world, although it contains everything, is the child of the mind. That is so wonderful.

I cannot understand why Jacqueline does not ask Blasius to tell her such things every day and to explain to her what she does not understand.

He is a dear boy and would do it for sure. I wish somebody were ready to teach me. Indeed, Mr Pascal and Blasius and Aunt Marie are very nice to me, but if I asked Mr Pascal or Blasius to explain such things to me, they would think I was mad, because such a thing is not for maids. We maids must never forget our place in society."

She stood close to Blasius' writing desk, staring motionlessly at the maze of lines. The lines started to curve more and more, until there wasn't a single straight one; then they blurred and turned into a picture in which a young woman stood in a garden, surrounded by three children. The children resembled the woman to such a degree that it was apparent she was their mother. She had also the feeling of having seen the woman somewhere before. The more she made an effort to see the face of the woman clearly, the more blurred it became, until it dissolved completely. She took a clean handkerchief from the deep pocket of her full skirt and wiped away her tears. The picture disappeared and morphed into clear lines again. The big gilt case of the table clock caught her eye; Blasius kept it on his writing desk all the time to remind him, by its soft but steady ticking, that he shouldn't waste his time.

She moved the clock towards the edge in order to free the desk from even the tiniest of dust specks. On the usually shining upper side of the case she noted a fresh water stain. With her handkerchief she wiped it off and polished the surface to a good high gloss.

The face which she saw in it could not be distinguished from that of the woman whom she had seen just a few moments ago. In the shining upper surface of the untiringly ticking clock the children were absent.

"Nevertheless, there is at least one thing they can never take away from me: I may always dream about it," she spoke to herself quietly; pride and impotence mingled in her voice.

"If I consider it further," she continued with her thoughts, "intellect and the world determine themselves, while they determine each other. I am delighted by the dream of falling up the waterfall. And if I consider this even further, I come to the conclusion that both the waterfall as well as the one who is falling, in fact, hurryingly rest. Oh, all that is so fascinating. I wish I could hear such things every day. I could never get enough of it. But I am only a maid, and such things are for clever people, not for maids."

"Louise, hurry up please!" Aunt Marie's voice interrupted her daydreaming.

Aunt Marie and Jacqueline were in the hall downstairs. Only now she also heard the voices of Blasius and his father, who had just returned.

Louise called that she was coming. She cast one last glance at Blasius' drawings on the writing desk.

"Could I dream without my everyday life?" she asked herself.

Then she hurried out of the room.

*

Lunch did not last long, because in the household of Etienne Pascal one was not in the habit of feasting for hours as was customary in distinguished households. Meals as well as all other things were just seen as something necessary and had therefore no ritual significance. Thus immediately after lunch everybody withdrew and went to do their favourite activities: Louise cleared the table, Aunt Marie retired to her room to have her afternoon nap. She was frail and fragile by nature and needed a rest after lunch due to her rapidly approaching old age. Jacqueline and Gilberte also withdrew to their rooms where they indulged in absolutely different passions.

Gilberte looked at drawings of the latest models of ladies' clothes, thereby engaging in the favourite pastime of many young ladies from affluent families. The drawings came from the hand of a certain Monsieur de Plussale who hailed from a neighbouring country. Since his earliest youth he had barely been interested in the opposite sex, but more in the clothes of the opposite sex.

He always created new models, new shapes, new possibilities. He was heartbroken that he had to sleep and eat, and believed every hour in which he did not design ladies' clothes to be lost time.

He was jealous of his customers who acquired his popular clothes at high prices and would have loved to wear his creations himself. He dreamed of wearing them all at the same time and of showing off to his clients in order to make them livid with rage. He wore his hair slicked back and gathered in a ponytail at the nape. Rumour had it that he had undergone an operation to get rid of a specifically male appendage which was responsible for facial hair growth and hair loss in men in order to retain a thick mane of hair and to resist the process of ageing. Unfortunately his face got covered with countless little pimples only a few weeks after the operation, resulting in a multitude of tiny scars that left his face rough, albeit beardless.

This man did not like his name – he used to be called Dirtier - so he decided to change his name upon his arrival in the city of fashion and elegance. The naughty municipal office employee working on his case, who spoke French as well as the couturier's native tongue, suggested to him to take Plussale as his new name, because it sounded much better. The latter did not understand any French, so when the joker put a 'de' in front of his new name, explaining to him that it wouldn't necessarily be of any financial benefit to him, but that it would definitely grant his person due style and elegance as well as enable him to get access to the highest social circles, Monsieur de Plussale didn't have any reason whatsoever to hesitate.

Now all the distinguished slender ladies of Paris dreamed of his clothes, but only the richest among them could afford them. Poor ladies could, of course, spare themselves such tormenting dreams.

Monsieur de Plussale was proud of the fact that the distinguished women desired his clothes, because it was due to them that he was somebody, though at the same time it hurt him very much that they wore his dresses, because he thought their bodies unworthy of his creations. This caused him to be torn apart by both pride and envy at the same time, two emotions that rivalled each other in their intensity and made him a gravely ill man. Despite all that, he couldn't have imagined a more interesting and fulfilling existence than his own.

Jacqueline read a thick book of legends about the lives of Saints, who were an inexhaustible source of inspiration to her. There she also found ideas for her poems that she intended to dedicate to the expecting Queen.

Some time before, Blasius had started joining his father in his study more and more often after lunch, where they sat discussing things for a long time. They always had a lot to talk to each other about, because seven years had passed since they moved from Clermont to Paris, and Blasius had turned fifteen. His knowledge in the fields of mathematics and natural sciences, and also his general knowledge, had already prospered so far that he was up to any conversation. In most cases he deemed even discussions with scientists as not particularly demanding. This day he again went to his father's large study.

There they sat opposite each other in the comfortable armchairs, eating grapes – it was once again early autumn – and spoke firstly, as usual, about all kinds of physical and philosophical problems, then passed on to questions of a different nature.

"I would like to put a question to you, dear Blasius," Etienne Pascal turned to his son, "and at the same time ask you to give me a sincere answer."

Etienne Pascal knew his son well. He knew that Blasius would never lie to him; this time he didn't doubt his son's frankness either. He knew, however, that Blasius was an exceptionally sensitive chap and, despite his extraordinary mental abilities and his serious take on life, only a child.

He also knew that Blasius loved and revered him and that he would do anything not to hurt him. That was the reason why he didn't want Blasius to suffer or hide his suffering in order not to cause him, his father, any grief. Blasius was a special, highly gifted child with a sense of respect and sympathy and, hence, he asked him to speak frankly, because he thought first and foremost of the happiness of his child and not of his own. That couldn't have been any other way, for Etienne Pascal found his happiness in the happiness of his children.

Blasius on the other hand would never be insincere towards his beloved and above all admired father; causing him grief was the last thing he would think of. He listened to his father with undivided attention.

"The eternal wanted," his father started, "your dear mother – she was an angel on earth – to leave us so early. Why she had to go, I do not know, and it is not in the competence of any person to know such a thing."

"Oh, dear father," Blasius interrupted him, "I don't know exactly what is happening in your soul, but I can have a vague idea about your feelings. Our mother must have meant infinitely much to you, and I am sure she would have meant no less to us children."

"You are perfectly right, dear Blasius, because she was ready to live for others. By doing so she lived for herself. Her approach to life was different from that of other people's and she drew the strength for her life from the knowledge that any other person was herself. She was in the habit of saying that, and she did not only say that, she also lived what she said. Everyone who knew her admired her for her attitude and behaviour."

"Gilberte, Jacqueline and I," replied Blasius, "were too young then to be aware of all the love she had for us. When she left, we did not feel her absence. Aunt Marie has done her utmost to fill the gap. We call her 'Auntie', but the feelings we cherish for her are probably those that children cherish for their mother."

"The fact that Aunt Marie could come to join us," Etienne Pascal continued, "is, dear Blasius, again a part of the unfathomable providence of the eternal. Without her help our lives would have been much harder and we might not even be alive today."

"Your generosity and your patience, dear father, exceed all expectations; we children will never forget that."

"As you are no longer a small child, I should like to ask you whether the absence of your mother depresses you. I ask you this, because paternal love is not motherly love."

"No, dear father, I do not feel our mother's absence, because you with your love and goodness have made it possible for us children never to feel her absence but merely know about it."

"Thank you for your kind words. Your answer gives me a feeling of peace and the strength to hold out. When you speak, I hear the voice of your blessed late mother. You are her child and my son."

Etienne Pascal had said something that had triggered an urge in the boy to ask a question.

"May I ask you something, dear father?"

"Speak, dear Blasius, what can I do for you?"

"I have thought about it often, but now I would like to hear your opinion on it", said the boy, almost shyly.

"I am very curious, go on!" his father encouraged him.

"You have just said: "Your blessed mother." What do you mean by that?"

"A blessed person is an actually rich person."

"And who is actually rich?" asked Blasius.

"Only somebody who has something he can never lose is actually rich. One can lose money and material goods very easily, and, in the end, one must lose them when one dies. They are continually being lost, every second, by those who sacrifice their whole life to these disloyal companions. They are disloyal, because they change their owner repeatedly.

They stay longest with those to whom they are of no use, because as long as one has them, they are of no use, and when they are of some use, when one gives them away in return for something useful, one has them no more. Such wealth creates false happiness and true grief. That which one doesn't lose when giving it away is of real value and thereby one's most faithful companion."

"And what is that?" Blasius asked impatiently.

"It is insight. It is the only thing that increases each time when it is given away. Insight never gets lost, it can only be won. He who gives it away gives the most expensive of all gifts. It is the only precious gift; all other gifts are more or less fake gifts, which one must lose sometime, at the moment of death at the latest."

"And the blessed?" asked Blasius who had not forgotten his first question.

"The blessed are those who own the real wealth, who cannot lose anything, because they unintentionally carry the most precious thing with them at all times, so they needn't worry about anything".

"Does that mean that the blessed live happily in the hereafter as well?" asked Blasius, because he felt he was not understanding what his father was trying to explain to him.

"Only those, dear Blasius, who become blessed in this short, strange human existence also remain blessed for good. He who does not become blessed here, does not become blessed after death either. Only he who in this world lives already in the hereafter, lives forever and needn't wait for a hereafter after death. He who waits for the hereafter after death can't be let in and must remain outside. The blessed takes everything along to the other side before dying, precisely when he attains the insight. He builds his everlasting home, his everlasting native country there during his short fleeting existence here. No mote gets lost for him. The normally rich, the owner of the fake wealth, loses everything he has piled up, because he has devoted himself to many transient things, however, he never felt the eternal One, the essence of everything. He loses at the moment of death everything he has piled up during his lifetime, erroneously regarding it as his possession. What he has piled up is all he has and knows, and that is exactly what he loses. His empire and his wealth disappear with him. And because he then ceases to exist, the gate between time and eternity remains closed, for there is nobody to knock on it. The condition for the gate to open is that somebody should knock on it. Bliss, dear Blasius, is wealth which cannot be seen but only felt within oneself, which, however, ultimately means everything."

Etienne Pascal had finished his explanation, and for a moment the welcome silence hung in the air.

"Thank you, dear father, for this marvellous explanation; you are indeed the best teacher. Now I feel that I understand lots of things much better. Our mother lives through you in us children, and through the sense of your words she lives everywhere and forever. Only now do I understand what insight can do: it preserves from downfall without preventing it."

"So it is, dear Blasius. The idea you have just uttered will induce someone someday to write it down to make it fully-fledged. Then it will spread out its wings and fly out, clearly perceivable, into the world, where it will always exist, however, only as something extremely rarely known. Remember, dear Blasius: this thought is the eternal foundation of the world; if this thought is lacking, the world is but a passing."

"Oh, dear father, now I understand! If the fledgling does not leave the nest, both the fledgling and the nest must vanish!"

"Yes, dear Blasius, there is a time for every purpose, and so everything happens when its time comes. If the brood dies, everything before and after the brood dies, too."

"And one can learn when it is time for something to happen only when it has already happened, in hindsight so to speak," Blasius added.

"How are you getting on with the conical sections?" Etienne Pascal asked the boy, changing the subject.

"Well, very well, I have found a true chest of treasures in the cone!"

"I can believe you, the cone is a beguiling shape!"

"Yes, it is something absolutely delightful! It is the love child of the point and the circle line, a farewell to the shadows of the plane and at the same time a memory of it."

"Tell me more, that is thrilling," urged Etienne Pascal, almost dazed by his son's beguiling explanation. He had never heard such a thing before.

"The circle turns into the body if the centre and the circular line get married to each other. The child of that union is the resulting body."

Etienne Pascal was all ears, understanding a lot, however not everything that Blasius was telling him, because what he heard were daring and absolutely new, strangely expressed ideas. He loved intellectual challenges and new intellectual models, though only if they didn't refer to politics, where he abhorred any kind of change.

What Blasius was telling him was delicious food for an alert mind and a lively imagination like his.

"And how is the child of that union born?" pressed Etienne Pascal.

Blasius was happy to be able to please his father and continued with his explanation.

"If the point in the centre of the circle leaves the plane of the circular line, it touches a new plane, and that's how it happens."

"Would you tell me more precisely, please," asked Etienne Pascal.

"The birth of the point in the centre of the circle occurs when it leaves the plane of the circle and founds a new one. That is at the same time the birth of a body, of a new world, of our world, which can oscillate. And thanks to the fact that it can oscillate, it can experience and be experienced."

Etienne Pascal listened to his son with delight. The birth of the point out of the plane of the circle, this purest abstraction resulted in the concurrent birth of the body, of the concrete world, of that which determines our life down to the tiniest detail. For only the body can oscillate, and all that can be experienced is pure oscillation; the experience itself is but oscillation.

For his mathematically and scientifically endowed mind that was a unique pleasure. A boy was sitting in front of him, his own son, dainty and pale, a frail and delicate body, however, a source of most daring thoughts, fruits of a brilliant mind.

"Your explanation is very good indeed. Your blessed late mother spoke in a similar way. She, too, could express the craziest ideas and the strangest thoughts simply and effectively, just like you."

Blasius reacted to his father's words by continuing with his explanation,

"In that moment the centre and the circle line of the former circle are both separated and connected by the body of the cone."

Etienne Pascale was experiencing the most beautiful moments of his life. His young son made him feel the presence of his beloved wife who had been taken from him so early and as if by an inexplicable order that had come from an unknown realm. And this boy, the child of the invisible mother and his still discernible body, this living, speaking, thinking, feeling connection between there and here, sat in front of him and uttered the most daring and most peculiar thoughts he had ever heard.

"The picture of the dead, lifeless circle," continued Blasius, "which knows only one possibility and doesn't allow any alternative, gets ennobled, becomes a strange body resembling a horn, which knows basically three states: in one of the three states it can be divided by endless numbers of planes into two corresponding halves; in another case it is divisible by one single plane into two corresponding, but not congruent halves; in the third case it can't be divided into two corresponding halves at all. In other words it knows all states of the world experienced by us, where we now and then have the impression that endless analogies exist, sometimes only one, and sometimes none. In the case when it is symmetrical infinitely many times, it rests in itself and has a calming effect."

Etienne Pascal could not quite follow this thought, because what did the number of symmetries have to do with rest or calming effect?

"Why calming effect?" he asked Blasius.

"All distances from any point on the circular line to the top at the other end are either equally short or equally long, and everything is in perfect balance. Then the point of the horn is not bent to any side, because it has the same distance from all points on the circle line. In that situation nothing enjoys any privileges nor suffers any disadvantages. Then there is nothing that could tease more than something else. It is a state of balance bearable only by somebody who is capable of detaching himself from the tangible things and directing his gaze upward. Only then the princess resides in the very top of the glass mountain, waiting to meet a suitable life companion," answered the boy.

A smile of satisfaction flitted across Etienne Pascal's face.

"Oh yes, now I know, it's the third brother who manages to get to the top! Only his horse's hooves adhere to the steep, smooth glass flanks; only he has the chance of following the most difficult and at the same time the most important of all paths."

Etienne Pascal said exactly the same thing the boy had intended to tell him, thus proving to be the model pupil of the model teacher, who for his part had up to that very moment been the model pupil himself, and who now – in accordance with the rhythm of the course of events – continued to bring forward and develop further all that had already made remarkable headway. And because his father had said everything, the boy merely added: "It is the dreamer."

Etienne Pascal nodded to confirm that he had understood everything that concerned the quiescent aspect of the cone.

"And if it is simply skew?" he asked his young teacher for another explanation.

"If it is simply skew," continued Blasius enthusiastically and contently, "then it is enticing and divisible by one single plane in two mirror-image halves; then there are a longest path and a shortest one leading from the princess who lives in the point and hence claims no space, that is from where virtually everything converges, to the circular line where everything must be separate. The longest path and the shortest one lie in the only plane which can divide the cone simply symmetrically. Then each point in one half has its corresponding point in the other half. However, halves as a whole can't be made congruent, just like the right hand and the left hand."

Every new one of the boy's ideas increased Etienne Pascal's interest, because he felt elevated to previously unknown realms of thought.

"Ah, that is indeed amusing!" was his spontaneous reaction.

Blasius felt the seal of approval from someone he appreciated most. He remembered how crystal clear the mathematical explanations of his father had been when the latter had taught him the art of arithmetic, and now he explained higher things to his brilliant teacher, who had turned into a brilliant student.

"And between both these extreme paths leading from the circle line at the one end of the cone to the point at the other end," continued Blasius, "there are infinitely many possibilities, and endless number of paths; and each possibility is covered twice, making it a double infinity of possibilities as it were."

"The persisting duality," Etienne Pascal cut in enthusiastically.

"Our way of experiencing the world, split in two, between the two extreme paths, the longest and the shortest, our way of existing," added Blasius.

"And if it is twice skew?" asked Etienne Pascal further.

"If it is twice skew, it is completely asymmetrical; the circle is stretched to an ellipse. The direction of the inclination corresponds in this case neither to the direction of the long nor to that of the short ellipse axis, and then there is no possibility to divide it into two equal halves; then the shortest path between any point on the ellipse and the point where all the paths converge is in each case unique. This is at the same time our simplest conception of the world, when based on pure intellect and according to which even every smallest element must be different from any other smallest element. It is the conception of a world which is made up of unique solitary entities, each one of which has to take its own path to the top to which all paths inevitably lead," Blasius explained.

"That is the personal feeling of being an individual," Etienne Pascal added.

"One is tempted to say that the cone offers a simple analogy of our entire intellectual world view," said Blasius, beaming.

"How astonished the members of the Academy will be when they get to read the works of a boy," said Etienne Pascal, smiling proudly.

"I am happy, dear father, that we children don't annoy you," said Blasius, seizing the moment to find out whether the education of his children was a burden to Etienne Pascal on top of his already very strenuous and exhausting workload in the state service or, despite that, a very rewarding enrichment to his life.

Etienne Pascal's eyes filled with tears.

"Dear Blasius, please don't speak like that! Since the death of your dear mother I have never had an easy life, but your sisters and you have helped me experience the highest levels of happiness amid the utter grief. I am grateful to you for this gift of happiness every minute of my every waking day."

The boy noticed that his father's eyes were shinier than usual and that his voice was trembling. With his dainty, pale fingers he touched his father's well cared-for hand. It was clean and distinguished, without even the tiniest mark of dirty work whatsoever. Never before had he looked at his father's hands carefully, let alone held them in his own. He felt a light pressure and a gentle shake. Etienne Pascal looked his son in the eyes, but no word escaped his lips. For a short moment both were quiet.

"Only you, dear father, need to be thanked for everything," he spoke, because he felt that he had to say something.

"Probably neither me nor you, dear Blasius," answered Etienne Pascal.

His voice and the way he held his son's hand were full of suggestions inviting speculation. Blasius directed his look, which until now hadn't been directed at any specific object, to his father's face. Only now did he notice the numerous wrinkles lining his father's forehead. Those two between his father's eyebrows were particularly conspicuous. His father's eyes were filled with tears, and his Adam's apple bobbed up and down several times.

There they sat, father and son, holding each other's hands and looking each other in the eyes. That which connected them and held them together was his father's most treasured memory, and the boy before him, who understood and was capable of unbelievable things, was the gift of his memory. The boy did not share his memory; he had no emotional connection to his father's dearest emotions. Between him and his father's most precious recollection stood the father himself as the only connection between him and the mother whom he didn't know, but whose child he was, flesh of her flesh, blood of her blood. As he couldn't share his father's recollections he identified the goodness and the quality of his mother, whom he knew only from the portrayals of his father, with those of his father, whom he knew and revered unlimitedly.

"But to whom should we be grateful?" he asked his father.

While asking his question, he noticed at the same time something in his father's expression that seemed to say that it was not possible to express in words who or what deserved to be thanked, because any name would have been partial and therefore invalid.

"I sense, dear Blasius, that you are appointed to find out who we should be grateful to," said Etienne Pascal after a short silence. His face was blank.

"Father!" said the boy loudly, almost shouted; surprise and fear mingled in his voice.

There was no answer from his father, for in that same moment, Jacqueline entered the room. Her expression was serious, and her voice sounded excited.

Jacqueline's sudden appearance interrupted the strange conversation between father and son. Their hands slid apart spontaneously, but lay side by side on the table, so that it appeared that they had been lying very close all the time though always apart.

"Father," said Jacqueline, "two men of the Ministry of Finance are here, they want to speak to you."

Etienne Pascal remained still for a moment. He was probably contemplating the reason for this visit, for he hadn't been expecting it. A vague notion overcame him, but as he had never thought of that possibility, he tried to expel it as best he could, but it sneaked back in through the back door and stayed in place. He was sure of one thing: it would not be a pleasant visit.

"Tell them I am coming," he said, pretending calmness.

Jacqueline left the room nimbly and closed the door behind her.

Blasius had noticed that his father was not pleased with the unexpected visit, but he couldn't think why.

"What do they want, father?" he asked, somewhat timidly. However, he felt that his asking was justified, because after his conversation with his father he knew exactly what his sisters and he himself meant to his father. Besides, he had the impression that the time had come for him to take on part of the burden and responsibility that his father had to carry alone. Being acquainted with the matter was already the first step in that sense.

"I have protested against the new financial order

concerning the city's treasury. I suppose it is about that," said Etienne Pascal without thinking.

He was glad that Blasius wanted to know what it was about, because now he felt stronger and no longer alone. Blasius remained quiet for a moment and then said in a very low voice, almost suspiciously: "You have protested?"

He spoke that way because suddenly a father he didn't know stood before him, a father who could protest. There were no more tears in Etienne Pascal's eyes, and the conviction of having taken the right course of action emanated from his every word.

"Yes, I have and always will protest against all innovations and changes."

Blasius listened and couldn't believe his ears; just a few words had made him see his father in an entirely different light. It was as if he had two different fathers.

"But why is the new order so bad?"

Etienne Pascal stood up, because what he wanted to say was almost a political speech of a somewhat riotous nature.

"If the court wants to get even more money from the impoverished urban population in order to enable an even more excessive lifestyle for all parasites, then I view even the Royal Family, whose loyal subject I myself have always been, as my biggest enemy and the enemy of us all," he said with a determination Blasius had never known in his father before.

Blasius was dumbfounded. How could he reply? Before him stood his venerable father, a high official of the state, from whom he drew his high salary, high enough to afford an expensive estate and a comfortable life for himself and his children, and now that man, his father, protested; was a rebel who did not shrink from calling the Royal Family his enemies.

"But father!" Blasius said in a low voice, fearful that someone might hear what they were speaking about.

"Dear Blasius, you have heard me right. I shall go downstairs and find out what they have to tell me."

Though Blasius was taken aback and feared bad consequences, at the same time he loved the rebellious trait in his father's character. His father's attitude was a sort of a rebellion and adventure and besides, he tried to protect the poor and sided with justice; that was how he had understood his father's words.

This was to him something completely new and intriguing. He knew what he had to do straightaway. He had to eavesdrop on the conversation his rebellious father was about to have with the two men and later discuss everything with his defiant begetter.

"Nothing will escape me," he thought, "I must keep at it until the end."

With his mind set to learn everything he dashed out of the room and ran down the stairs.

***

The house in which Etienne Pascal lived with his relatives was spacious. Apart from the three children's rooms, a room for Etienne Pascal himself, a room for Aunt Marie, a room for Louise and a guest room there was a large reception room connected to Etienne Pascal's study by a sliding door.

Whenever he had visitors, this door remained shut. Now Blasius used the room behind the locked door as a hiding place from where he could listen in to the conversation between his father and the men from the Ministry of Finance. He had barely managed to sit down by the door when he heard the two men enter the reception room.

Etienne Pascal received them with habitual deference and asked them to have a seat.

"Mr Pascal," said one of them, probably the senior one of the two, "we are here by order of the Minister of Finance."

His voice sounded calm and matter-of-fact, and his posture was that of a perfect state official. He was not he himself, but just a conscious element of an immense apparatus; he didn't want to be anything else, he couldn't want it.

"The Minister of Finance?" answered Etienne Pascal, feigning surprise.

"Yes, actually the King sent us, but by order of the minister," said the younger official.

"And on what matter, if I may know?" asked Etienne Pascal, still pretending to be surprised. He was concerned, and he knew he should be, because he had to be prepared even for the worst. He himself was an important and respected state official; therefore he knew the rules of the game. The state system created privileges for its members and protected them, but in return it expected from them unconditional loyalty. If it felt betrayed by any one of them, it tended to punish the traitor particularly severely to give off a clear warning signal to all potential traitors.

"Your statement regarding the latest financial order has caused lots of anger in the Ministry."

"I see, I see," said Etienne Pascal, still pretending to be calm, "have you come to arrest me?"

"Yes, and no, Mr Pascal," said the junior official.

"So what is this all about?" asked Etienne Pascal with slight annoyance. "You either have been given orders to arrest me or you haven't," said he, "anything in between is impossible."

"Maybe for you, Mr Pascal," answered the senior official, "but not for the state, let alone for the Crown; they have intermediate stages of punishment for their subjects."

He spoke in a clear, firm and sovereign manner, the way someone speaks who is aware of being backed by somebody who has supreme power and in whose name he speaks and whose actions he justifies.

"I understand," said Etienne Pascal. "What am I supposed to do?"

"You aren't supposed to do anything, Mr Pascal; but we have just been sent to give you a piece of advice."

"What kind of advice?" asked Etienne Pascal trying to appear as self-confident as possible, because he had understood from the words of the junior official that he did not have to fear any serious danger.

"We have been ordered by the Minister to inform you that you have been removed from your present office as president of the Cour des Aides of Clermont," said the senior official.

He said it in a calm, straightforward manner; there was neither anger nor gloating nor any kind of excitement in his words. He would have probably spoken in a different manner if he had been sent to tell Etienne Pascal that the latter had been elected Minister.

Etienne Pascal was thunderstruck and sank back into his armchair. What he had just been told wasn't nearly as bad as being thrown into jail, but it was nevertheless bad enough, because it meant bidding farewell to all the advantages and privileges granted by the status of a higher state official. The loss didn't concern so much his own person, because he knew what he was worth, but rather the future of his three children, the most important concern in his life.

"Will that be all?" he asked, his voice broken.

"In fact, yes, however, there is one more thing which the Minister has asked us to tell you."

"I am listening," said Etienne Pascal barely audibly.

"The Ministry and the Crown are aware of your excellent work, your dedication and your moral values," said the junior official in a tone which was meant to emphasize that Etienne Pascal could not be replaced and was still considered a member of the apparatus of state, although he had made a bad mistake, and that there was still a small door open for him, should he some day decide to ask repentantly for forgiveness.

Etienne Pascal knew that repenting and returning back into the arms of the system one had previously been punished by meant a complete and unconditional weakening and humiliation of the repentant.

"I feel honoured," he said with a touch of irony, for he

didn't have to fear any further consequences, because what had to happen, had happened.

"Hence, we advise you, Mr Pascal," continued the junior official as if Etienne Pascal hadn't made any remark, "to leave Paris immediately by order of the Ministry and to take up residence in Rouen."

Etienne Pascal had heard what he had to be told. Now he knew where he stood and could therefore speak freely.

"You said my merits and my values were appreciated, didn't you?" he asked.

"The Crown and the Ministry agree on that," the senior official chimed in, as if asked by the Ministry and the Crown to express their fear they might lose Etienne Pascal.

"If that is really so," continued Etienne Pascal in the same tone, "why has my opinion regarding the latest financial order not been accepted? After all, it is the expression of my moral stance and my sense of duty to my fellow citizens."

Etienne Pascal's remark was clever, but the officials remained unperturbed.

"That is the way of thinking without intermediate stages, Mr Pascal, mathematical logic as it were."

For the first time in his life, Etienne Pascal heard that mathematical logic was not necessarily the best way of thinking.

"And what is bad about it? The matter is as clear as daylight!" He felt he was right, because now he was defending something that was right, not only according to common sense but which stood in perfect correspondence with the purest thought and as such had to be viewed as indisputable.

"Undoubtedly, Mr Pascal, undoubtedly, but clarity is a

virtue of mathematics. The authorities prefer ambiguity, because they always prefer to have an additional possibility of interpretation in stock, a free route as it were, in case they come under pressure."

The official had voiced what Etienne Pascal had wished to hear – the mischief; however he had said it without any scruples or blushes, so openly and so calmly that his words seemed to express rather the necessity of the practical existence than that which Etienne Pascal had wanted to hear. Thus a situation had been created in which Etienne Pascal had to explain something so obvious and self-evident that it didn't need any further explanation.

"But such an action can endanger the existence of the entire kingdom and must therefore be prevented by any means," he replied.

He appeared to be ridiculous to himself, because he was trying to explain to state officials and make them understand what was in the interest of the apparatus of state as if they hadn't known all that. He knew, however, only too well that they were aware of each detail. It was like trying to explain to a mathematician that a sphere was round.

"We do agree with you in the name of the Ministry and the Crown," the junior official remarked.

"By the way, there are a lot of places – perhaps everywhere in the entire kingdom – that would welcome such an attitude."

Now Etienne Pascal could understood even less which opinion the two men represented: did they speak in the name of the Crown and the Ministry or were they expressing their own views? He couldn't understand why clarity was not welcome everywhere.

"And why not Paris?" he asked in a loud voice, thus hoping to get a clearer answer, because everything seemed increasingly absurd to him.

"Paris is different and must remain that way," said the senior official calmly and patronizingly.

"Everything comes together in Paris and everything has to be possible here at the same time. Paris is both the country's heart and brain. In Paris theories and models, values and virtues should just be formulated, but they should be put into practice in the provinces, that is, by the majority of the population," added the junior official.

"You want to say that some should speak about virtues, fix them and put them into words, while others, the vast majority, should respect and put them into practice! What is the meaning of all that?" asked Etienne Pascal, looking at the men almost reproachfully.

"You, Mr Pascal, seem to have a sort of trouble-free, intact world in mind, don't you? That is dangerous, Mr Pascal, very dangerous!" replied the senior official.

Etienne Pascal felt that the tables had been turned on him and that the officials had regained the moral high ground. He did not understand the world any more, for how could people be reproached for wishing to create a trouble-free world? That was, however, exactly what the two state officials did; they were people who, if judged by their position, undoubtedly belonged to the most reliable members of the entire system.

"A trouble-free state should be dangerous? Where everything runs smoothly?" Etienne Pascal said, using clear logical arguments in an attempt to make the two officials change their opinion.

"Indeed, Mr Pascal, that's what it is. The state with problems makes life hard, we know that only too well, however it is the most fertile ground, the only one on which a healthy officialdom as a social stratum can prosper. No problems, no social strata, this would be the worst thing that could happen," the junior official instructed him patiently in a tone of assuring spontaneity, so that he himself no longer knew who had uttered more nonsense, the two serious, smartly dressed civil servants or he himself, also a respectable, smartly dressed civil servant. He could not understand how their opinions could be so different from his, for they belonged to the same social class and should therefore protect the same interests. He didn't know any more whether ultimately the whole thing was but a misunderstanding. However, he knew exactly what he had said as well, as that the two officials were not mentally retarded but rather very clever people. Therefore he couldn't understand how the two men could support such absurd ideas.

"Couldn't it..." he made a feeble attempt to clarify the confused conversation and any misunderstanding that might have arisen, however, the senior official cut in on him immediately and didn't allow him to finish his question.

"Mr Pascal, we all know what you have to say. But if there weren't any problems, neither you nor we, neither the king nor the decree would exist; we wouldn't speak to each other and nobody would waste a single word on us. On top of all that, the wish, the desire to attain a state without problems wouldn't exist any more. Thus we all would lose the will to live and the right to exist!"

What the senior official had said at a stretch sounded

strange yet peculiarly convincing, and Etienne Pascal felt overwhelmed by a strange logic that was beyond him.

Though he would never have doubted the rightness of his attitude, however, he did have to admit that the system and the tactics of those in whose name the two officials were speaking were so clever that he, a clear-thinking mathematician, could not contest the validity of their assertions. They made no sense, but they were extremely effective.

"The troublemakers are indispensable for our life, is that what you are trying to say? Woe to those who happen to attain a trouble-free state! Am I right in my assertion?" Etienne Pascal spoke in such a tone, because he didn't know any more how to defend his opinion.

"Those who some day might happen to be about to attain the trouble-free state wouldn't experience either happiness or woe, because they would disappear before attaining that state. We all would disappear, because a state without problems would be too much, unbearable, deadening. Problems are the powerhouse, Mr Pascal, they are the basic prerequisite for the existence of the world," the junior official said, trying to teach and enlighten Etienne Pascal. The latter became increasingly irritated, because he didn't have any suitable arguments to put pressure on his opponents.

"And we are here to deal with such problems, am I right?" he asked, clinging to the last shred of hope to untie the two men from their mad, absurd attitude to life.

"Certainly, Mr Pascal, we are here to come to grips with problems and thereby maintain the world. It is not easy, but with some resoluteness the problems can be contained, not solved mind you, but kept within limits. A reasonable stock of problems is always desirable, not too many, not too few, but just a reasonable stock, a healthy balance. Keeping that reasonable stock occasionally requires enormous effort, especially when the insurgence of the wild mob can't be suffocated by any other means except by power. Only in such moments it becomes obvious how important loyal and capable officials are," the senior official said, and while he was speaking he didn't stir. His face remained calm and there was no sparkle in his eyes, no twitching of his facial muscles, no wrinkles on his forehead. Even his lower jaw hardly moved. Only his thin lips, which resembled two barely visible brushstrokes, fused to one thin moving line when he spoke. What Etienne Pascal heard was uttered by those lips. The rest of the official's face didn't participate in his speech in any way whatsoever.

*

Blasius was sitting in his hiding place behind the door and listening to the strange conversation. He could make out from the words of both officials who they were, who they must have been.

"Officials are only necessary because there are problems," he thought, "otherwise they would be superfluous."

Though the two visitors defended a view which seemed to be in stark contrast to his father's, he nevertheless had the impression that they somehow went together. Even all three voices were so much alike that Blasius had an impression of only hearing his father's voice. On the one hand his father's ideas seemed to him desirable, yet somehow also suspicious. The way the two visitors saw the world, on the other hand, seemed hideous and degrading to him. Above all he could not understand that a being gifted with intelligence could be content with such a moronic activity and such a superficial way of life.

After a short interruption he heard his father's voice again.

"In such moments they are, we are, necessary, important, indispensable ... yes, yes, yes, only in such moments."

Blasius peeped through the keyhole and tried to see the faces of the officials, but he could only see his father, because the key was in the lock and the tiny gap offered only a very small field of vision. The two visitors were not visible so that he had the impression that his father was talking to himself, performing a sort of depreciatory hand movement and shaking his head with resignation. Then he heard his father speaking slowly and in a very low voice.

"To give credibility to their statements ..." Etienne Pascal spoke to himself in an almost unintelligible whisper. "In order to give credibility to their statements they impertinently work in philosophical quotations, which they have picked up somewhere. Thereby everything seems to have a paradoxical air of wisdom. Or could they be right after all?"

"Where would we be if everything was in order?" asked one of the officials again.

"Consider that carefully, Mr Pascal. No problems means nobody is needed to solve them. The officialdom as the most important social stratum would disappear instantly. With them would also break the main pillar, the backbone of the state. Do you know, Mr Pascal, what that would entail? Can you imagine the most terrible of all scenarios?" the junior official said, and every word he uttered sounded well-thought-out, had its own logic and corresponded to reality.

Etienne Pascal, who loved clarity and clearness above all, felt that the words of his visitors were basically senseless, but he did not know with certainty where the contradiction in their lines of thought was. He rested his forehead in his palm and looked at the ground.

"No, I can't imagine that," he said sincerely, for how could a state without problems be imagined when nobody in the entire history of mankind has ever known such a state? The same also applied to the periods without state officials, because even human societies without a real state featured certain members who lived at the expense of the majority but who were nevertheless considered to be indispensable. He felt that for the people who had grown up in a world with officials, a state without officials had to seem inconceivable. For such a state Etienne Pascal's imagination was not vivid enough. Therefore he answered the official's question in the negative.

"We are not surprised, Mr Pascal, because handling the state affairs requires more, infinitely more, than the usual one-sided way of thinking of mathematics. It always requires the ability to take into consideration all steps between yes and no. It requires looking ahead and glancing backward at the same time. It never permits that on the ladder of history both hands are held free simultaneously. One hand has to hold fast the rung at chest height while the other tries to reach out for the next higher rung at forehead height. In the same manner one foot must stand firmly on a lower rung when one tries to put the other foot on the next higher rung. That ensures that each rung is experienced as something new, because it is separate from the previous one. At the same time one should be aware that each rung contains certain elements of all previous rungs, because it is connected to them by means of bars."

The official's harangue about looking forward and glancing backward, innovation and continuity, bars and rungs, separation and attachment made Etienne Pascal's head throb so strongly that he almost had a headache, and asked himself whether he had ever been a real state official. If he hadn't, what had he been then? He was just an amateur mathematician; furthermore he was one who put his mathematical knowledge in the service of the state, which on its part made him a state official. And now he had the feeling that the end of his officialdom was nigh.

"Now I do understand well," he said, after the official had finished his explanations.

He said it to get rid of the strange visitors. He had worked too much during the few days before, none of which could put more than twenty-four hours at his disposal, and now he needed a rest.

"We are pleased, Mr Pascal," said the senior official in a tone, which simply expressed their satisfaction that they had done a task successfully.

"We advise you," he proceeded in the same tone, "to leave Paris immediately. This is the middle course which has been chosen for you. Putting you in the Bastille would mean neglecting your previous merits. On the other hand not punishing your criticism of the government's policy could encourage others, living and those to come, to do the same. Punishments are there to educate, education to prevent future punishable offences and thereby decrease punishments."

He spoke in a superior style, considerately, friendly and cruelly at the same time. Etienne Pascal could detect all that in the official's words.

"How much time do I have?" he asked in the way of a convict who knows he has got off with a mild punishment.

"See to it that you are gone by tomorrow morning at the latest."

Etienne Pascal felt that the friendly advice weighed more than any strict order.

"We are glad, Mr Pascal; we wish you a good journey. By the way, Rouen isn't at all a bad town. In addition, nobody knows that you have gone there. Everyone will believe that you are already in the Bastille. That belief will undoubtedly help people to resist their bad temptations. Good night."

That was all the officials wanted to tell Etienne Pascal. It wasn't a long sermon, however Etienne Pascal had been told everything. Although he himself was an experienced, respected state official, he felt more like a junior student in a school in which the strange skill in managing public affairs is taught. The senior official added his personal "Good night" and the two men from the Ministry of Finance immediately proceeded towards the exit. Etienne Pascal stammered a shy "Good night".

The visit was over. Blasius left his hiding place and stepped into the reception room. Nothing pointed to the fact that just a few minutes before an extremely strange conversation had taken place between the state system and one of its parts, because the part concerned had decided to behave no longer in the way prescribed by the system. However, because the part concerned was a capable one, the system had decided not to destroy it, but instead to grant it one more opportunity to find its way back.

The part seemed to have understood the language of the system.

***

Etienne Pascal learnt a lot from the conversation with the two officials from the Ministry of Finance. He thought about it countless times, linking together the officials' ideas, and the more he pondered upon them, the more sense they made to him; he discovered some logic and a connection in all their statements, although at first everything they had said had appeared utterly irrational and despicable to him.

When he had to leave Paris, he thought the two officials were two evil messengers who spoke and acted in the name of a monstrous system. Nevertheless he had not forgotten one thing, the fact that he had not been jailed, which could have been expected, because his attitude carried the seeds of subversion and was an immediate menace to the authority of the state.

Now, however, because some time had passed and he with his people had gained a foothold in Rouen, the explanations of the officials seemed to him to be something that had to be supported as soon as one had recognized the essence of the system as such. Both officials were, after all, his colleagues, they even worked in the same Ministry; however, at that time they were much further ahead, much more advanced in the art of running the state than he himself. The state appeared to him as a necessity, neither good nor bad, but simply as something indispensable, even when present in its most cruel form. The people as individuals now had, in his opinion, the single purpose of serving the state which made them into what they were: gregarious animals equipped with a little intelligence, which wouldn't be able to survive without the strict hierarchy within the state structure. Was that not sufficient proof that the state as the form of organisation of human society would never cease to be a necessity which people would never be able to do without, as long as some were more capable than others? Only if people should some day find the ways and means to abolish such differences among them, the state would stop being a necessity, he thought.

The state thrived due to the differences which caused tension among people; however, at the same time it made them dependent on one another by assigning them their places in the ranks of the hierarchic structure of society. That was neither good nor bad; it was just the way it was. Within that ranking order everybody had some scope, some more and some less. Those at the bottom dreamed of a higher airy rank – somewhere closer to the top – with more possibilities and more freedom and were consumed by envy, desire and the struggle to move upward. Those in the higher ranks with much scope and freedom did everything to prevent anyone from attaining their own status for fear of losing their own advantages. Thus they were consumed by that strange struggle as well. Therefore both groups filled their lives with making the other party's life harder.

The hierarchy as the basic pattern in the body of each state structure incited the members of society to dream of a goal and to struggle to attain it. In other words it offered them a raison d'être.

If that was the case, then what arguments could be brought forward against the state as the organized form of human society?

Etienne Pascal's flights of thought ended there, because he was not able to give any answer to that question.

Sometimes he had the impression that such a struggle was a sufficient reason for existence. At other times it seemed to him not quite convincing that such a life was what man deserved. However, the question of what man actually deserved appeared to him to be no less problematic. All people before him, countless millions of them, had been put into the world and had lived in various societies, and each society knew a ranking order. Now he also lived with all his contemporaries in a similar, clearly hierarchically organized society, and the future didn't promise anything else. Man was still at the level of gregarious animals, with the only difference that he had the means, unknown to the animals, which enabled him to maintain the hierarchical order as the basic pattern of social structure. Physical strength was no longer decisive as it was with animals, and neither was pure intelligence, but a specific way of thinking.

Up to this point everything had appeared to him to be clear and plausible, but what was that specific way of thinking which assigned the prestigious places in the ranks of power in human society to those who were successful? He was not completely sure about that, although he now and then had the impression that it was, after all, the hideous ability to despise others; not the ability to hate, mind you, but the ability not to respect. Hatred paralyzed, because it destroyed one's own draught-horses. Disrespect however, allowed for, even promoted, condescending friendliness, thereby creating the necessary building material. In his considerations he usually came to the conclusion that those who hated only rarely harmed others, however, always harmed themselves. Those who didn't respect others, on the other hand, walked over the bent backs of the vast majority as successful personalities of outstanding merit. Sometimes they happened to step into the gaps between the bent bodies of the inferior many, experienced occasionally even a short shock, however, they soon pulled themselves together again and continued hopping resolutely and indefatigably on the backs of the not respected ones, passing along the torch of success. They never failed to see to it that the trivial people, the *canaille*, under their feet were thoroughly acquainted with the memorable past in which the successful few were to be remembered gratefully and held in awe.

*

Etienne Pascal lacked nothing in Rouen. A stately home was available to him and his people, and thanks to his respectable income everybody under his roof could enjoy a comfortable life. He wasn't the president of the revenue office of Rouen, however that had hardly any influence on his pecuniary circumstances. As once in Clermont, he was now by far the most mathematically gifted official in Rouen. In addition, his inventive son had constructed a calculating machine so as to help his beloved father do his work with less effort. He regarded his calculating machine as one of his greatest achievements. In order to prevent other people from having the idea of copying his machine and then claiming the copyright, he familiarized several influential personalities with his invention. In conversations with his father, but also at other occasions, Blasius expressed the conviction that his invention could be technically surpassed and he himself could build a better, faster and more efficient one within a month if he had some skilled craftsmen to help him. What, however, could never be surpassed, he claimed each time in a declamatory manner and with a raised index finger as if threatening, was his invention itself, which, he said, could some day in the future create possibilities that his contemporaries couldn't even dream of. He saw, he said, a time coming in which his invention would determine virtually all aspects of interpersonal relations, so that someday people would no longer need each other at all. From a technical point of view his invention was just the beginning, however, as an idea it was the end, because it was to substitute people and make them superfluous in all fields. There was only one task left for man: to serve his invention.

Etienne Pascal had that sort of conversation with his son almost daily. His son's invention enabled him to do his work in the revenue office of Rouen much faster than before, while other employees had to remain in the office and barely managed to cope with the calculations. He anticipated a new era heralded by his son's invention and it was only a question of whether the world they lived in was ready to realize the scope of his invention.

*

When the two officials from the Ministry of Finance informed him that he had to leave Paris he had been barely able to contain himself. Now, however, he lacked nothing, and he had no reason to complain. In addition, the fact that he was not president in Rouen and had to work more instead of giving orders, made his son build a calculating machine which would, according to the inventor himself, one day radically change the entire world.

On the one hand he was proud of his son's invention, which made his work much easier; on the other hand, however, it made him feel something he couldn't quite put his finger on, but which he carried around as a feeling and a wish: may such a thing never be given to the world.

"It is good that we left Paris in time," once he told his son in a conversation, "otherwise they would have locked me up; the Bastille is not there just for looking at. It is easy to get there; however, it is quite difficult to get out of it. And if that happens, it is in most cases too late."

"But would they really have locked you up?" asked Blasius with surprise.

"Undoubtedly", said Etienne Pascal, "why wouldn't they?"

"Why do you think so?" Blasius wanted to know, because he could not understand how his father could speak about such a thing without the slightest trace of anger or excitement.

"Because the state as it is has to be on the alert."

Etienne Pascal's words unleashed a feeling of dismay in his son.

"On the alert?" he asked in surprise and looking stern. "But against who, father? Nevertheless, you have always been a loyal citizen, a friend of peace and order!" he complemented his question with the comment as if he wanted to help his father find a proper answer. His words concealed his feeling of helplessness.

"You are right, dear Blasius, I have always been loyal, and I have always supported law and order and thereby I have supported the privileged, because law and order are of benefit only to them. The underprivileged don't benefit from it at all. Without exaggerating, one can say that law and order are the arch enemies of the poor and the best guarantor that everything must remain just as it is. Hence it is easy to understand why the underprivileged always demand equal rights. If equal rights existed, they say, they would have nothing against law and order."

Blasius listened to his father attentively. Everything he heard was clear to him and it was hardly possible to contest it. However, he missed in his father's words a clear opinion which of the two were right, the privileged or the underprivileged. Therefore he asked his father to explain that to him.

His father's answer wasn't in anyone's favour.

"Both the privileged and the underprivileged are right and wrong," he said.

"How should I understand that, father?" Blasius asked him after a short but complete silence.

"The underprivileged are right," continued Etienne Pascal, "when they demand the same rights, because they are deeply convinced of being disadvantaged. They would also like to have a comfortable life!"

"That makes sense to me," interrupted Blasius, because what his father had just said was clear to everybody and didn't need any further explanation. He could not understand why the privileged were right, too, although they demanded the opposite. He feared his father might evade the problematic part of his question.

"But when the privileged ..." he wanted to continue but was interrupted by his father, because Etienne Pascal had already realized what his son was about to say.

"When the privileged demand law and order, they wish to go on having a comfortable life. A change of their situation would, in their opinion, be bad for them. Both sides want to have a comfortable life, and although either side has a different stance, both of them want the same."

"I have understood that, too, but I still do not understand why both sides are wrong."

The idea that either of the two sides was right appeared to Blasius like an object in front of a mirror; however he was not able to project the image of that object into the mirror.

There, in the mirror, everything had to be completely upside down and yet so correct and convincing that it could serve as a reference when decisions were to be made in everyday life. What was that completely upside down and yet completely convincing picture like?

Etienne Pascal had noticed what he owed his son. It was not simply about a purely intellectual affair which he could have dismissed with a clever answer, but rather about something that could be of major significance for the future life of his son. For that reason he tried to articulate his answer as simply and as clearly and above all, as convincingly as possible.

"Both parties are wrong," he said quietly and sensibly, "because either of them demands something that serves only its own interests but doesn't pay heed to the interests of the other side."

The boy seemed to have understood what his father wanted to say, but he was not satisfied with his answer, because he didn't like compromises made in desperate situations.

"What could be done?" he asked his father, because he personally didn't know the answer to his own question.

"Certainly not very much, dear Blasius," Etienne Pascal answered, shaking his head with an earnest expression on his face.

The serious expression of his honoured father, who he thought of as the cleverest, or at least one of the cleverest people alive, taught him that even the brightest minds with great experience could be as helpless as someone of his tender age in view of the difficulties that arose from human beings living together. He realized that everything had to be the way it was but he couldn't accept it, because he thought that people should have the means of dealing in a sensible way with the difficulties life brought about. If people were incapable of that, then there was just a gradual difference between them and animals. In that case people were on the same page of the book of life on which all other creatures were to be found.

"And why not?" he asked his father, hoping to receive at least another partial answer which might bring him a little further on.

"Because there is no impartial judge who could say what is right and what is wrong," answered Etienne Pascal without stopping to reconsider his words even for one single moment. That pleased the boy, because he had not expected such a prompt answer.

"Is there really nobody in the world who can say clearly what is right and what is wrong?"

"There is no lack of such people, but there is nobody among them whom both the privileged as well as the underprivileged would like to have as a judge; either he appears desirable to one party or to another or to neither of them. Somebody who is genuinely desired by both parties is beyond the reality of everyday existence. Therefore all Messiahs must fail. They can cause a lot of turmoil but not free the flesh from troubles. In the end every born Messiah must get drowned in the unfathomed ocean of human wishes. Only the Messiah who is being awaited is the living one."

The boy felt he understand the situation: people were divided into two camps, and the gap between them was unbridgeable. Those in one camp were deeply convinced they were underprivileged, deprived, exploited and oppressed and were thinking about how to change their situation. Those in the other camp knew that they were privileged, the exploiters and the oppressors and looked for ways and means to maintain the existing situation.

It was, of course, hardly conceivable that, as matters stood, anybody could be a suitable judge. But he hoped that his father might know an answer to even that.

"Is there really nobody in the world who can say clearly and satisfactorily what is right and what isn't?" he repeated his question with a great expectation in which hopes and doubts balanced one another.

In spite of his extraordinary intelligence the boy's voice sounded naive.

"Indeed there are, but a judge can only point to bad things, however, not doing bad things does not depend on the judges but on the goodwill of those who do them. Their particular lifestyle is the cause of such bad things and for them at the same time their main purpose and meaning in life. To renounce their bad ways would mean about the same thing to them as to renounce life; no judge could ever ask that much from them," answered Etienne Pascal.

"Father, does that mean that justice will never prevail?" Blasius asked, now a little more quietly and more soberly.

"That's the way it is, dear Blasius. That can never happen, because everybody sees justice from his own point of view. Indeed, there will be attempts to introduce justice for everybody, but those who perhaps have very serious intentions must in the end inevitably become criminals, creators of a new, more delicate injustice which hides behind fancy names and forms, rides on the majority's back, causes hardship and sows the seeds for future sufferings."

Etienne Pascal spoke calmly. There was something prophetic in his words and therefore not even the slightest trace of regret about the fact that people would never be able to establish a community without animal hierarchy, in which nobody feels the need to oppress and exploit others and in which every individual experiences the destiny of each other individual as one's own, and makes the greatest possible effort in order to help any other human being in need.

"Father, does it mean that everything will remain as it is now?" the boy asked.

The ephemeral joy had disappeared from his face, and his question resembled more a cry for help.

"Basically everything will always have to remain the same; however, the practical realization of the same will be different each time: oppressors come, do their foul work for a while and then they have to go; however, the oppressor and the oppressed will not disappear as long as people live like animals in hierarchically organised societies."

"Your picture of people and their world is very bleak, dear father. I have always thought that in their inmost soul human beings are good and that it is but the circumstances that make them bad."

"Oh, dear Blasius," said Etienne Pascal, now completely relaxed, sincerely and openly, "so-called good and so-called bad respectively in human nature is a very strange thing."

"Tell me more about that," Blasius asked, in the hope of getting to know a little more about the essence of the human being and then perhaps to understand better the irrational behaviour of God's noblest creature.

"The so-called good," continued Etienne Pascal, "know very well how despicable their conduct of life is, but they don't try to change it. They instead excuse their hideous actions by blaming some early ancestors of man who reportedly had done something that they should not have. As descendants of very sinful ancestors they declare themselves basically sinful. They also declare their heavenly lord omnipotent, infinitely good and gracious. After having equipped and adorned their celestial lord and master with all infinitely magnificent qualities, they can expect from him forgiveness for all their wrongdoings, because they didn't equip him thus free of charge. Being such a marvellous, infinitely gracious and merciful lord, he has no other choice but to forgive them all. Thus the so-called good ones seem to be well acquainted with the best strategy for attaining eternal salvation: they declare themselves to be sinful monsters and their heavenly master to be omnipotent, infinitely gracious, merciful and forgiving; thereby the celestial lord gets blackmailed by his sinful creatures in a very subtle way. Being the celestial lord with such qualities, he has no other choice but to forgive them everything. If he fails to do that, he loses his divine attributes. That is the strategy of the so-called good. It allows them to commit all kinds of crimes and to act just as they please without having a bad conscience."

The boy listened to his father carefully, trying not to miss anything his father said, because his father's words were extremely important to him as guidelines he wanted to follow.

"If I understand you, dear father, then the creators and founders of religions must also belong to the good ones?"

"That's right, dear Blasius, they are the pillars to which their good followers tie their boats to be sure that they can never be called to justice for their hideous way of living."

"And the so-called bad?" asked the boy, full of curiosity.

"The so-called bad ones see no difference between so-called good and so-called bad deeds. They don't think of changing their hideous conduct either. Instead, they create all kinds of models in which everything is dissolved into the smallest elementary particles. Such elementary particles can be neither good nor bad. And because people are – like everything else – composed of such particles, they cannot be guilty."

Etienne Pascal had arrived at a point in his explanation where one had to interrupt him if one had listened to him carefully, because he was talking about guilt and innocence in human life.

Blasius had listened attentively; hence he interrupted his father with the question of why nobody was guilty.

"Because the smallest element is a neutral thing in itself," answered Etienne Pascal.

The boy was all eyes and ears, for such thoughts concerning the issue of guilt and innocence couldn't leave an alert mind cold.

"Please explain that a bit more exhaustively," he asked his father.

"Only when a smallest particle pairs with another smallest particle do all kinds of roles as concomitant complementary elements of our practical world come into being. Then we speak of charges, of polarity, of the opposite or the complementary, depending on what we want to say."

Etienne Pascal's words ended in an avenue with trees growing on both sides, many marvellous, venerable trees, each of which could have been regarded as the most interesting one. For the same reason none of them could claim universal validity.

Blasius wasn't happy about this, because it didn't make sense to him that many different things and ways could be right at the same time, although they presented themselves to the mind as pure opposites. Such a thought seemed to him strange, even dangerous.

"But, dear father, is there any single principle which one should live up to in order to act and live righteously?" asked Blasius, desperately yearning for a satisfactory answer, like someone languishing for water in the desert.

"Yes, there is one, but it is too high," answered Etienne Pascal without the slightest hesitation.

"Is it something people already know about?" asked Blasius with some relief, because if such a principle existed, he was ready to live up to it at any cost. The reward for a virtuous life was so great after all that no trouble should be shunned to earn it. That was the teaching of the holy church to which he as well as his clever father belonged.

Etienne Pascal answered promptly.

"The wording itself is generally known, however, its content is too high for almost everybody. Therefore it is not suitable and, in fact, worthless!" he continued in a calm tone.

Blasius had not expected such an answer, for if his father thought of that principle as unsuitable and worthless, then it had to be something formulated by some special individuals, however because of its uncompromised purity it was for the vast majority impossible to follow if people wished to lead a so-called normal life.

In order to follow that principle, one had to abandon the usual way of living and all normal values completely and tread on the path of loneliness up to the last breath.

"And what would that principle be?" he asked his father, his young voice trembling.

"Do to no one what you would not like to be done to you," said his father, uttering that ancient instruction for a righteous conduct of life which is so general that looking for its author would be but a futile business.

"That is the core of morality," he added, "the only one; everything else is just hypocrisy."

"Why is everything else hypocrisy?" asked Blasius.

"The hypocrites always appeal to foreign judges and authorities or to the infinite mercy of the supernatural being invented by them, thereby trying to push the responsibility away from them. This high principle, however, forces every individual to self-consideration and self-judgement: in short, to a way of living up to the standard present in one's own heart; that doesn't need any external standards or authorities."

"Father, do you think that some day human beings will be able to adhere to this principle?" asked Blasius, hoping for an affirmative answer.

"Your question, dear Blasius, lacks precision, and therefore it is not possible to give a precise answer to such a question."

"And why is my question not precise?" asked Blasius, because he did not understand what his father meant to say.

"Because the concept 'human being' needs a precise explanation before this question can be asked."

"How should I understand that?" asked Blasius, full of surprise that such a simple, usual question could be vague and maladroit.

"Only he who can follow this principle *is* a human being, a true person. All other conducts of life are at best the preliminary stages of the human being, the way thither, however, not yet the goal."

"If that is so, then there are few people in the world, although there are countless organisms that call themselves people," replied Blasius, adding his own remark to his father's answer thus inciting further consideration of the question.

"That's exactly how it is, dear Blasius. The eternal has not yet woken up – it is still slumbering in all those who cannot follow this principle. Such are in the vast majority. Therefore there are a thousand times fewer people than one believes."

"Isn't it enough to make you despair, dear father?" asked Blasius with an earnest expression.

"It is unimportant how many of them there are, hardly worth mentioning," answered Etienne Pascal. "If there is one single true person, the true human being exists. If the true human exists, the hidden eternal has woken up and is alive, and the world is holy, the expression of everlasting meaning, in spite of all."

"One single person can give the whole world its meaning?" asked the boy as if he had not heard properly. He, in fact, wanted to gain some time in order to digest what he had just heard and to accommodate it duly in his youthful, innocent view of the world.

"That is exactly how it is: only what can happen, indeed happens. What can happen, however, every individual learns only in retrospect, after it has happened. Thus every person experiences the past as his present. That is the nature of the comprehensible world. Therefore each person is aware of his own world, which only happens in him and for him. That personal world is for each individual everything, the entire world. Thus everything that can happen for an individual happens in that particular person. That person is the place in which a complete world takes place. Therefore, finally, only somebody who is aware of that is responsible for everyone. The ignorant are innocent and have no responsibility."

"Each single person in possession of this knowledge is responsible for everybody?" asked the boy once again in the same voice and with the same intention, because what he had heard was not easy to digest and contradicted everyday experience and usual practice. According to the usual way of thinking nobody was liable for some unknown people's deeds.

"Yes, dear Blasius, everybody who finds the meaning of life has found it for everyone, because everybody lives a different way of life to any other person, and that different way of life in any other person makes the latter the other person. We ourselves are the others; each of us exists as many times as there are others."

"Dear father, does that mean that I am any other person and that any other person is me, that I live in all other people and that all other people live in me?"

"You have said that splendidly, that is exactly how it is. The one in whom the eternal wakes up has the responsibility for all those in whom the eternal is still slumbering."

"But does he not first and foremost have responsibility for himself?" asked the boy, still uncertain whether he had properly understood his father's words.

"The person in whom the eternal has woken up does not need to look after himself, and he indeed does not do that, because he is, safe, protected, in good hands. His only concern is the happiness of the inhabitants of his own house, the variations of himself; he rescues them from drowning in the meaninglessness of the raging time-stream, thereby saving the world and becoming the Messiah without being aware of it."

***

The conversation between Etienne Pascal and his son was suddenly interrupted when a young man burst into the room and declared, without a greeting, that he wished to speak to Etienne Pascal. His wish was uttered in such a rough way that it sounded more like an order.

Etienne Pascal asked the unexpected visitor why he had entered the house without an invitation.

Louise, who had followed the visitor up the stairs, now appeared saying that she had opened the front door and asked for his name as usual to announce him, but that he hadn't paid any heed to her and had run upstairs straightaway. After that she withdrew into her room.

It was very obvious that Etienne Pascal was angry, because he deemed the young man's intrusion into his private space to be rude at best.

However, the visitor's clothes and demeanour made him react calmly. The young man was clad in the appropriate uniform of a courier and his stance was erect and upright, his hat under his left arm. He was holding a letter addressed to Etienne Pascal in his right hand.

The letter bore the seal of the Chancellor.

"What do you want?" asked Etienne Pascal. His voice wasn't friendly, but it remained matter-of-fact.

"The Chancellor himself has sent me; I must speak to Mr Etienne Pascal urgently!"

"It's me, tell me what you want."

The courier stretched out his hand with the letter.

Blasius found the unexpected visit and the tense atmosphere irritating, and asked his father if he should leave the room.

"No, stay here," said Etienne Pascal, because he wanted

his son to participate in all he knew or did.

"This letter is for you; the Chancellor is expecting your immediate reply," the courier said.

Etienne Pascal took the letter from the courier's hand. He did it very slowly, as if trying to guess what the letter might be about before opening it.

It was undoubtedly about something extremely urgent and important.

Etienne Pascal looked at the seal for a moment, opened the letter carefully and scanned the lines quickly before asking the courier to wait for a moment, because he would like to read the letter undisturbed.

No sooner had Etienne Pascal called Louise than she appeared and he asked her to take care of the courier.

*

Etienne Pascal read the letter once again very slowly in order to be completely sure of having understood its content correctly. His face took on a serious expression. Blasius didn't fail to notice it and asked what the Chancellor wanted, without waiting for his father to speak.

"The Chancellor is in danger and needs my help urgently," said Etienne Pascal.

"The Chancellor is in danger?" asked Blasius with surprise.

"Yes, he is, that means we, all of us, are endangered," said Etienne Pascal.

"All of us?" Blasius asked, still very surprised but now also with a worried expression on his face.

"Who do you mean when you say 'all of us', father?" he

asked, because he couldn't understand why his father should be endangered yet again, for the highest authorities were obviously interested in his father's well-being and serving of the state.

"We and people like us, people from well-ordered backgrounds," answered Etienne Pascal calmly.

"But who is threatening us?" asked Blasius, because he still couldn't grasp where the threat was coming from.

"Who? Ahem, who?" Etienne repeated his son's question, not knowing what to say, because those who threatened were at the same time the desperate.

"Yes, father, who?" Blasius repeated his question, because he had noticed that his father hesitated with giving an answer.

"The same people we depend on," Etienne Pascal answered calmly.

He would have preferred not to answer the question; however, he knew that it was impossible, because Blasius wanted to know the true state of affairs, and, apart from that, he was too intelligent to be fobbed off with a naïve answer.

"And who are they?" asked Blasius directly, so that there could be just one clear, satisfactory answer.

"The plebs, those who ceaselessly clamour for equality and the same rights for all. Equality can't exist; they want to seize the power! And if they seized the power some day, it would simply change hands – that's all; but then there wouldn't be equality either."

Etienne Pascal was expecting a reaction to his explanation, however Blasius didn't comment on it.

"What does the Chancellor want from you, father?" he asked, as if it had been his first question.

"He wants my support," answered Etienne Pascal.

"And what are you going to do?" asked Blasius.

"We can't just give in, authority is not a prostitute, it deserves due respect," answered Etienne Pascal in a relaxed and resolute voice.

His father's words made Blasius feel thunderstruck, because what he had just heard did not fit the picture he had of his father.

"But, Father!" he almost screamed.

"Yes, please?" replied Etienne Pascal calmly.

After his son's loud and excited words Etienne Pascal's voice sounded even calmer than it actually was.

"Do you know any of those who are protesting?" asked Blasius, convinced he was right and his father wrong. He was absolutely convinced that his father contradicted himself.

"I don't need to know any of them; single individuals are not important. I know one thing for sure: all of those who protest are cast in the same mould. They are all the same bunch."

"What do they have in common?" asked Blasius, because his father's opinion seemed to him to be too personal, too unfounded, too unadvised.

"They all disagree that disorder is mankind's greatest enemy," said Etienne Pascal, in the same calm, lecturing manner, like someone whose appointment and life-task was to save the world from chaos.

"What are you going to write to the Chancellor?" asked Blasius, trying once again to get a clear answer.

"I won't write to him at all," was his father's completely unexpected answer.

"And why not?" insisted Blasius, not allowing his father a single breather.

"Instead of writing I'll go there myself," answered Etienne Pascal resolutely.

"You are going there? But isn't that dangerous?" asked Blasius, now slightly alarmed, because he hadn't expected that his father might intend to go there.

"Dangerous or not, I must go, I must help him, I must help us, I must help everyone!" replied Etienne Pascal resolutely.

"You must help everyone?" Blasius was astounded, for he didn't understand anything anymore. He could well understand that his father wanted to help the privileged. But how could he help the poor when he was acting against their demands?

"Of course I will, I must help everyone," said Etienne Pascal and stood up from his chair. He wanted to leave.

"If you want to help everyone, do you also want to help the poor?" asked Blasius, still mainly out of curiosity, however his question sounded slightly accusatory.

"Yes, I do want to help them by showing them their place and thus freeing them from all sorts of bad temptations. It is important to know one's place and never to try to transgress one's boundaries."

Etienne Pascal spoke clearly, declamatory, emphatically as if playing the role of the Chorus in a Greek tragedy. Then he called Louise, the maid, and asked for his coat. She appeared a second after she had replied that she was coming and helped her master and employer put on the fine quality garment. Etienne Pascal buttoned up his coat and left the room without uttering a single word.

Blasius stared through the closed window into space.

The loud banging of the front door shook him awake out of his thoughts. His father was gone.

*

He sat down in an armchair, threw back his head and closed his eyes.

"I have some difficulty in understanding my own father," he mused.

"He has always been infinitely patient, caring, mild, gentle and understanding towards us children. Now I have the impression that he would be ready to sign death sentences, although those he wants to punish have never harmed either him or anybody else. They are but the suppressed thirsting for equal rights. My father says equality doesn't exist. That may be true, but being equal and having the same rights are two different things. That all of us are different does not depend on us nor is it of much significance. However, that all people have the same rights is of greatest significance. Does he not understand that or is it me who misunderstands everything? He himself has protested against the ordinance of the Ministry and the Crown. That was the reason for his beating a retreat to Rouen in order not to end his days in the Bastille, languishing among rats and spiders. Now he won't tolerate the protest of others. How should I understand that? The only difference between his protest and the one of the plebs – as he calls them – is that he is against a change, and they demand it. He demands law and order, and they demand relief from their misery. But he himself has said that they are both wrong. Then he is wrong, too. But wait a second. He has also said that they are both right, so that makes him right, too. That is really of no use as an explanation. But there is another possible explanation: he knows that the masses are also right, however he and those like him are more right because they are cleverer and therefore have the situation in better perspective.

Well, that might be true, but what good is my father's intelligence to a poor sod? After all, his intelligence serves the interests of the King and the mighty state machinery, even when he has to flee their wrath.

My father has taught me mathematics, the art of connecting separate elements with each other. Now that art is my possession, and I can't forget it even if I wanted to. I might be his son, mentally and physically, but there is something inside me that rebels against his stance. Can preserving a political system be the ultimate human goal and give meaning to life? I have some difficulty in believing in that. Perhaps I'll realize some day that something like that can be the final objective in life, however, I don't see it yet."

*

In his considerations, he had arrived at a point where it suddenly became clear that human behaviour could be neither understood nor explained by the mind.

He opened his eyes and leant forward.

"Oh, in mathematics everything is so clear; there are no differences of opinion, and if there are any, then they may cause a merry and exciting discussion in the worst case. The differences of opinion which refer to society end at best in a bad mood and at worst in bloodshed. In my opinion it is an indication and proof that all the so-called humanities are of little worth, because they are indeed not sciences, although they like being treated as such. However, even that may change some day, we are still in the process of fermentation, the wine is still lacking flavour, it is not time yet; every true thing has its proper hour and rejects any other one as a substitute."

While he was turning these thoughts over in his mind he suddenly happened to look at the clock and realized that a long time had elapsed since his father had left the house. The evening was already approaching, and a feeling of anxiety for his father crept over him, a notion that a new period of life was imminent; and every new period had to be preceded by a turning-point, a change of direction.

*

Etienne Pascal had departed in order to stop any change and preserve the status quo forever.

Was his action a direct consequence of his mathematical way of thinking? Perhaps, because mathematics was based on firm laws, and if mathematicians made errors, they did it not because the mathematical way of thinking was wrong but because they failed to use the mathematical way of thinking strictly.

Blasius also loved mathematics and very much so, but he could not understand why people should not look for new, more suitable forms of living together.

"States and political systems are nothing holy; they have neither always existed nor will they last forever. All of them have been created by bloody wars, which cost many an innocent life and brought privileges and comfort for the unscrupulous," he mused, tying one thought to another and for a moment unaware of the fact that his father, who was engaged in a dangerous task, hadn't returned yet.

He didn't know what it was but he felt that there was something that made his world view fundamentally different from that of his father, although both of them thought mathematically and appreciated clarity above all.

"I wish I could put my own father in the position of the disadvantaged just for a few moments in order to see how he would behave then. Of course he wouldn't be allowed to know that an experiment is being carried out on him," he continued musing.

In that same moment, however, he realized how foolish his last thought was, for it went without saying that his father wouldn't have been allowed to know that an experiment was being made on him, otherwise it wouldn't have been an experiment at all, nor would his father have belonged to the plebs.

A dismissive hand movement expressed his feelings in that moment. But then the chain of his thoughts continued again smoothly.

"I assume that he would then fight just as fiercely for equal rights. I can hardly imagine that he would then be against a change of the situation. If that, however, is the actual state of affairs, then we all have neither decency nor dignity, then we all are but scum, infinitely far away from the state that deserves to be called human beings."

His own thoughts had brought him into a canyon, which was becoming increasingly narrow, its sides increasingly steep and which ultimately led nowhere.

He put the palms of his hands to his temples and leant forward, so that now his gaze was directed to the ground in front of him.

"One could go mad," he whispered. Then it was silent again, because he didn't say anything more. He didn't hear the maid enter his room.

"Wouldn't you like to have your dinner, the table is laid?" she asked. Her voice was as gentle and friendly as ever. She didn't fail to notice that he was worried and tormented by something; however, she couldn't know what it was.

"No, thank you, I'm not hungry. I'd like to be alone for a while, I have something extremely important to clarify," he answered in a resolute tone and then added in a very low voice: "the crucial thing!"

Louise didn't say anything but left the room in the same manner she had entered it, making hardly any noise.

"For if these things are not clear," Blasius continued with his soliloquy, pronouncing some words audibly, "then mathematics alone is a mere confusion and a foolish entertainment of that tragic mash in our heads, of which we are so proud."

*

"Master, Master!" a loud voice shook him out of his thoughts.

It was the maid.

"Come downstairs! Quickly!" she shouted.

It was apparent from her voice that something extraordinarily unpleasant must have happened.

Blasius hurried downstairs towards voices that were getting increasingly loud as they approached his father's study.

Only a few moments after having left his room he was returning, followed by the maid and two men who were carrying Etienne Pascal on a stretcher.

"Here, on this bed, but carefully," he instructed the two unknown men and pointed at his father's bed.

"Don't worry, it's not our first time, we are in action every day, aren't we, Orlando?" said one of the two carers – that is what they appeared to be – to his colleague, a slim, somewhat nervous fellow with soft greenish eyes and curly black hair.

The word 'action' evoked in Orlando certain memories of his younger years.

*

At that time, Orlando tried whatever he could in order to become a dreamer, however, all his attempts failed, for he simply was not born to be one. His trying hard to become what he could not be made him suffer. He dreamt of becoming a poet and did whatever he regarded as typical of a poet. Thus he wore a beret-like cap and a cloak, because those pieces of clothing reminded him of pilgrims and wakened in him the desire to travel far away, hoping to find the sacred there. However, he never ventured to travel to some distant part of the world, because his fear of the unknown overweighed his curiosity to learn about it. Therefore, he decided to stay at home in the world he was acquainted with as a reasonable makeshift, however, to dress like a pilgrim there.

He had another secret heart's desire: he wanted to experience a real adventure, to be a noble hero who robs the rich of their money and helps the poor. He acquired two revolvers and a pair of leather boots that reached far above his knees. He used any time when he would be completely undisturbed to stage suitable adventures in his room. He put on his boots and his cap and wrapped his cape round his shoulders. Then he opened the wooden chest, in which he kept all the things that he loved and appreciated most, and took the two revolvers out of it. He held them firmly in his hands while aiming them at invisible travellers and ordered them in a deadly earnest voice to give him all the valuables they had. Each time he imagined different travellers, however a charming young lady never failed to be among them. Yet he never yielded to her sweet looks. Quite on the contrary, he wounded her heart so much that she blushed every time while she was slipping off the rings from her fingers and putting them gracefully into the leather bag he was holding before her. He enjoyed very much the wistful, longing smiles the young ladies granted to him, however he knew only too well that he had to resist the temptation to succumb to the charm of their eyes and that everything had to be under his control until the last moment. He could recollect very precisely many a beautiful young lady he had met in such a way. All of them remained faithful to him and were ready to be recollected by him any time he wished it – however, they shunned reality.

*

Something strange happened, however, one day. He had properly dressed and prepared everything as usual with the intention to ambush and rob the first travellers that happened to pass by. He waited and strived with all his imagination, however, in vain – no coach appeared.

This failure, which was only caused by the reluctance of the rich travellers to cooperate when he was waiting for them, kindled in him the flames of a fury he had not known before while they were ready to obey and act in accordance with his wish and imagination.

It was obvious that they did not take him seriously any longer. Therefore he had no other choice but to teach them a lesson and show them that he was not to be made fun of.

A week later he was lying alone in ambush by a country road and waiting with loaded revolvers for those who had thought him a poor fool with no other alternative but to play an audacious robber in his room.

After several hours he finally saw what he had been waiting for; a coach, driven by two splendid dapple-greys, was approaching.

When the carriage was some thirty yards away from him, he came out of his hiding place. He walked slowly, giving the impression of self-confidence and holding both revolvers ready to fire. He made gestures with one hand as if telling his accomplices somewhere behind him to stay hidden where they were, have the travellers in their sights and wait for his sign to act accordingly if necessary.

When he ordered the coachman to stop and get off, the latter tried to use his firearm. The would-be-robber, greatly hurt and humiliated, shot him on the spot, climbed onto the coachman's seat and tied the reins to the seat. He ordered the travellers to get out one after another, put their hands behind their heads, walk about ten yards away from the coach and stand there with their backs turned towards the coach until he ordered them to do something else.

The travellers did silently what he had ordered them, because they had seen what had happened to the coachman.

He found two little cases with money and precious jewellery as well as two firearms in the coach. After having emptied the content of the cases into a leather bag and stuck the two firearms in his girdle, he got out of the coach and ordered the travellers to get into the coach again. He ordered one of the men to climb onto the coachman's seat and to continue the journey immediately. He held his revolvers ready to fire and gave him to understand that the same fate would catch up with him if he tried to make the slightest delay.

Thus Orlando had received his baptism of fire and become a genuine highwayman. The inauguration passed smoothly, because a charming young lady was not among the travellers.

*

"That is exactly what we are," replied Orlando, "it must be like that, you know, because every day lots of people try to attain something, and every day lots of others try to prevent them from attaining it. Thus every day something happens that enables us to do something good. Am I right, Rusus?" said Orlando turning towards his friend.

"We are grateful to God for all that and we pray to him daily he may in future have mercy on us and all others like us by giving us the opportunity to do good."

*

Rusus, the other of the two carers, a stately, eloquent man of remarkable acting talent, nevertheless shy, nodded. In his youth, Rusus was no dreamer however, he knew what to do with the time he lived in. He indeed did use his time, but he did it in the most absurd way possible: he dealt only with the past all the time, because it was there that he found the world he liked. The consequence was that his present moments were filled with the past. He did not have any faith; however, he was very religious, which helped him later on to live as a pious criminal and due to the course of events to come to stay in Etienne Pascal's home.

*

"That's indeed how it is", Rusus cut in on his colleague, "and fortunately it is so, I must say, for if there were no clashes and conflicts, we would hardly get any opportunity to do good deeds. However, things as they are allow us to do good and thereby feel inside us the fruits of the holy teaching."

"How did this accident happen to my father?" Blasius asked, somewhat irritated, because the carers' words caused a sort of confusion in his head; what the two men said sounded on the one hand very religious and, on the other hand, it did not seem far away from deriding religion. Therefore he tried to change the subject.

"He addressed the crowds calmly, telling them that they wouldn't achieve anything by protesting and had better disperse; as well as that the state wouldn't tolerate that sort of behaviour. He told them they had half an hour to disappear, otherwise the army would restore order by force,"

Rusus said in a calm tone.

"And what happened then?" asked Blasius.

"A miracle happened," said Orlando.

"What sort of miracle?" asked Blasius, increasingly flummoxed by the carers' strange explanations.

"The crowd dispersed and your father was able to triumph," explained Rusus quietly with a touch of flattery.

"As he went to leave the platform," continued Orlando, "he stumbled over the Chancellor's walking stick, fell and broke his leg."

"That's exactly what happened," said Rusus and nodded.

"Luckily we were there to help. We tended to his broken leg, and now all your father needs is proper care."

"I see," said Blasius rubbing his forehead with his fingertips.

"Could you recommend some suitable people who can attend to my father adequately?" asked Blasius worriedly, because he did not know where to find suitable people

"I don't think we'll have to look very far for them," said the older carer to his thin colleague.

"We will not have to look for them at all," answered the other and a ghost of an impish smile flitted over his face.

"We would be pleased to take this task upon ourselves, and we know exactly what is needed," said Rusus in a calm reassuring voice

"Gentlemen, I am much obliged to you for your readiness and kindness," said Blasius, obviously relieved, although the two carers seemed quite strange to him. However, he did not have any reason for being afraid they might harm his father in any way, for they had obviously been doing their job carefully and correctly.

"Thus a huge problem has been solved," he said with an expression of satisfaction.

The two carers were no less satisfied.

"If it suits you, you can stay here right now," said Blasius to them and his voice betrayed that he was afraid the carers might unexpectedly change their opinion and leave, which would have put him in an extremely difficult situation. He suddenly became aware that there was a sphere of practical life in which he was not able to move at all, which, however, did not seem to be less important than the world of mathematical problems. The care of the broken limbs of the human body obviously required an entirely different skill.

"We have a large room which you can use during your stay here," he said in an extremely friendly tone and it was clear that he wished their consent. "It is next to my father's bedroom."

"That is perfect, because in these first days your father will need intensive care."

*

Blasius and the carers quickly agreed that they would take the care of his father upon themselves. Etienne Pascal being the person directly concerned had to say the last word. Therefore Blasius turned to his father and asked him whether he would like to be taken care of by the two gentlemen or whether he should seek other carers. Etienne Pascal was exhausted and spoke very slowly, hardly audibly.

"I agree; the two gentlemen seem to know their job; I have experienced that personally", he said.

"If that is so, we need not seek any further. Then everything is in perfect order. Only your opinion, dear father, can count here, for it concerns you. I myself am happy that suitable carers are immediately available," said Blasius contentedly.

Then he turned once again to both men and asked them whether physicians or additional carers would be required.

The younger of the two carers reacted to Blasius' question by punching his colleague in the ribs and asking him for his opinion as if he had not known in advance what his colleague would say. His colleague made a spontaneous evasive movement with the upper part of his body, although he knew only too well the intentions of his companion and did not have to fear a hit but just a tickle.

"Whether we should need help? Us? What for?" replied the other to his colleague's question.

"What physicians can do, we can do, too," he continued. "And what they cannot do, we are not supposed to be able to do either," added his colleague.

"What is known is known, and what is not known is unknown," his older colleague cut in on him.

"Doctors can help no more than we can," started the younger, a rather unhappy manoeuvre to support his colleague, "but neither ..."

He could not finish his sentence, because his older colleague had already anticipated the end of the sentence before his talkative young friend had uttered it. He gave him a light, discreet tap in the ribs to prevent him from further speaking and thus avert a possibly disastrous effect.

"We are talking too much instead of doing something!" he said in a manner intended to underline his zeal and assiduity.

"We'd better go and get our things from the carriage."

The way the carers spoke to each other and their furtive glances and gestures made Blasius wary; however, he ascribed it to their low education and their way of living. Therefore he was not worried about it as long as they were good carers, which indeed they seemed to be.

"Certainly, do that first. Your room will be ready soon," he said, for it was already quite late, and he wanted the carers to retire to their quarters before it was too dark.

After the carers had left, Etienne Pascal asked his son what he thought of the two men.

"What should I say, dear father, my knowledge of human nature is still quite limited, but in my opinion they are not crooks but rather a little uncouth."

"That's also my impression," replied Etienne Pascal.

"One thing seems certain: they know their trade," Etienne Pascal said, in a way as if trying to defend the two carers who, during the following weeks or perhaps months, were engaged to be his personal guardian angels.

"That is the only thing that matters and all we need," replied Blasius. He was happy that his father had approved of the carers and that he personally did not have to decide if they were the right people or not.

"I noticed one thing straight away," said Etienne Pascal to set his son at ease, because he had the impression that Blasius was somewhat worried.

"What is it, father"? Blasius asked curiously, almost anxious that his father would suddenly come up with something unpleasant to jeopardize the previous decision to keep the two carers. That would, of course, have had unpleasant consequences, for in that case he would have had to look for other carers, which seemed to him very difficult.

"Both men seem to be very religious," said Etienne Pascal quietly.

"Why do you think that, father?" inquired Blasius.

"Ahem, why? Before they fixed my broken leg, they repeated continuously 'Sweet Jesus, help us!! Sweet Jesus, help us!' Only strictly religious people speak that way."

"I have no objections against honest religiosity," replied Blasius.

"Neither have I if it helps, however …"

Blasius interrupted him, not allowing him to finish what he had intended to say, because his father's words suggested something undesirable.

"But father, why are you speaking like that? I have the impression…"

"The impression is wrong," said Etienne Pascal, "I am not faithless, not at all, but my religiosity is different and has nothing to do with the usual one."

"But, dear father, it goes without saying that everyone has a different religiosity and inevitably one's own religion."

"That's exactly what I meant, and for that same reason I have my religion. I do not belong to any one, although all the people who know me think that I adhere to the official religion."

"Then everything is in order. My first impression was that you are against religion," said Blasius.

"No, I am not against religion. Most people need a religion, and that will continue for quite some time. And because people need some sort of religion, it can do great service to those in power. That is why its importance should not be underestimated, even if one does not take it seriously at the personal level," said Etienne Pascal.

"Have you been able to help the Chancellor, father?"

"Help? Ahem. If I hadn't arrived in time, the plebs would have hanged him, that is how incited they were."

"They would have hanged him, you say? That is incredible."

"Yes, they would have hanged him, you heard it right."

"But why, father? That is the most brutal way of settling accounts with an extremely hated person. What has he done to them?"

"To fill up the treasury, he abolished all social services and doubled the taxes. That's why," answered Etienne Pascal soberly.

"But why does the state suddenly need so much money? Until now, the usual duties sufficed, and now, all of a sudden, double the previous amount is required! How am I supposed to understand that?"

"Well, the state always needs more than it has, that is its most important trait. The more it has, the more it desires. It doesn't necessarily need it, but it simply has to ask for more."

Etienne Pascal spoke quietly and very slowly in order not to exert himself too much. While speaking he was looking at the ceiling, his arms crossed. His last words provoked Blasius to ask more questions.

"And why must it have more and more?" Blasius asked. He wanted to hear an explanation of why the same state had to have more and more although it could manage well with much less money a while before. Furthermore, it was obvious that those from whom the state demanded more and more were bound to meet their doom, which inevitably meant the end of the state as well.

"Because it is a Moloch, a monster, which has only one innocent trait: it believes that it is indispensable."

Blasius did not trust his ears, because his father's words confused him thoroughly.

"But father, you call the state a monster, but at the same time you support it by helping to oppress the poor even more! How should I understand your stance? Father, I am desperate. I know you are clever and intelligent, but your behaviour seems cruel to me! Please help me to understand you!"

While Blasius was desperately stammering out his questions, he was standing, pale and trembling, propped on both arms by his father's desk. His gaze was focused on no particular object on the desk but was rather lost in its large pastel green surface on which countless documents had been written by his father's hand, which must have made the hard life of many people even more difficult.

After having directed his desperate questions to his awesomely admired father, he waited for an answer without stirring, but no answer came. He turned around and looked at the bed. His father was asleep, snoring quietly. Partly out of anxiety, partly out of despair and annoyance, because his question hadn't been answered, but also partly because he was not aware of what he was doing, he turned towards his helpless begetter and screamed, "Father! Father!" seeking for help from someone who himself was in need of help.

There could not be any answer, for Etienne Pascal was in the deepest chamber of the dream palace, where the intellect had no access. Before Blasius lay a helpless, immobile body and that which is usually called 'mind' was not in it any more.

"Oh my God! Who should I turn to now?" he whispered, sobbing, and lifted his head, his eyes fixed on the crucifix on the wall above his father's bed.

"Only there, where reason has no access, a satisfying answer and a way out can be found."

He arranged the soft woollen blanket on his father's bed and was about to leave the room. At the door he met both carers, who were carrying their utensils and in that same moment wanted to enter the room of the patient.

"Your father is very tired," said the older carer. "Fractures weaken the body. He needs much sleep and rest, at least one whole week. May we ask you to see to it that during this time your father is not exposed to any strain whatsoever? We and nobody else should look after him."

Blasius nodded approvingly, left the room noiselessly and retired to his quarters.

***

Blasius' room was very simply furnished. On entering one could see, besides a desk and a bed, only a wardrobe and three armchairs, one by the desk and two at the wall opposite the door. All the books he had were on his desk, yet there was enough room, so few were they. Beside the books there were a flask with apple vinegar, a simple small candlestick as well as a graceful crucifix, the pieces of which were so thin that they looked more like lines of a drawn system of co-ordinates than pieces; one could easily get that impression. Among about a dozen books which made up his tiny library were the Euclidean Principles, a Bible bound in leather and a volume of Essays by Montaigne. The rest were, without exception, books of the works of antique authors such as Homer, Sophocles, Virgil and others. No other objects could be seen in the room, no ornaments, no pictures on the walls, no flowers.

He was very tired, but that was nothing unusual with him, for he always felt exhausted; that was his permanent condition. Now he was so excited and confused by all the events and the strange behaviour and the words of both carers, but especially by the remarks made by his father, that he didn't think of going to bed yet.

He sat down at the desk in order to draw something precise in connection with his new calculating machine and to clarify how his invention could be improved.

A sheet of paper with conic sections on it was still lying on the desk, which surprised him, for he had taken away all the sheets the day before, because he had nothing more to say about them. Now a sheet was there, full of strange lines and signs, which diverted him away from his intentions and forced him, in the truest sense of the word, to meditate.

"I have studied the conic sections thoroughly," he spoke to himself, "and clearly formulated all laws and everything in connection with them. There is hardly anything else that could be added to it. The gentlemen in the Academy are thrilled; Fermat has also congratulated me. I have the impression that he is honestly happy about my scientific progress and so are possibly some others. Only one of the great mathematicians, who knows my work, seems to be envious of my scientific success. However, it is possible that I just have that impression. Whether he envies me or not, I cannot know for sure, however I know one thing for sure: I envy him! Yes, I envy him from the bottom of my heart! He snatched away from me a very important thing, perhaps the most important thing. His system of coordinates is worth more than all my mathematical achievements taken together."

His eyes remained fixed on the thin-armed figure of the cross. He took the thin metal object and began turning it slowly in his hands and inspecting it carefully from all sides.

The body of the crucified was extraordinarily thin and not separate from the two pieces standing perpendicularly to each other, but rather united with them to a single piece, thus resembling more a flat relief than an independent body. For a fleeting view, it was only a cross, for the body of the crucified was but a weak thickening of the pieces.

"Herein lies the secret of everything, and he was the first to notice it. No wonder, he is thinking itself. He can think so clearly that it is solely cogitation itself that he cannot imagine as non-existent. All others, me included, cling to appearances of clumsy reality. He moves smoothly in a world in which he does not need perceptible things. It is something incomprehensible to us. When I recently spoke to him in the Academy about atmospheric pressure, he said once again very clearly and unmistakably that nature did not tolerate the emptiness, although he was well acquainted with my experiment on Puy de Dôme.

Is he so stupid and so stubborn that he cannot understand it? He certainly is not. He is extremely clever, and when he asserts something, he has a reason for it, because he has an additional dimension in mind that he primarily means, which, however, is too hard for us to grasp. Toricelli and I rely only on the results of the experiments. Nature, however, seems to go much further, infinitely further."

An expression of sadness and impotence spread over his face and the whole room seemed to be filled with a unique silence – nothing stirred. He stayed quiet for a short while and could hear his own heartbeat and the rushing of the blood in his arteries. He had the impression the objects in his room had been listening to him and were now acquainted with his innermost feelings. His thoughts and feelings seemed to him no longer to be just his personal matter but rather something that suddenly belonged to everyone, even to those most distant in space and time.

"Now it is beginning to dawn on me what he meant," he continued. "Density is but one of the infinitely many ways of our experiencing the world. Nature seems to know all conceivable degrees of density; however, it shuns the absolute void. He is right, because the extremes like the absolute void and the absolute density are but models, creations of the human intellect. And because they are just models they cannot be reached in any way. For if the extreme were reached, everything that preceded the extreme would disappear; and because after the extreme nothing can follow, the entire world would disappear, therefore also the extreme. That is why these extreme models have no place in nature, but remain solely children of our speculations."

He placed the crucifix carefully on the desk, leaned forward, propped his elbows up on the desk and let his head rest in his palms. He sat like that in silence and felt defeated and miserable.

"In the opinion of the general public and in that of the scientific circles I may triumph," he thought.

"But Cartesius knows secretly that no other can share his deep insight. He is alone with his opinion, but he doesn't need any like-minded supporters. Now I have a gleam of hope that he is no longer the only one to understand why nature does not know the absolute void. When he looked at me with his large black eyes during the conversation, I had the impression he was somewhere else, totally absent. The conversation with me was not enough for him; at the same time he had another interlocutor, a much higher one, who he spoke to at the level of pure thought, without wasting a single word."

*

A sudden knocking on his door shook him from his thoughts, and all that just a moment before had made up their content disappeared into thin air, vanished.

"Come in!" he called in answer to the knocking of the unexpected visitor. The door opened and he saw the two carers.

"Come in, gentlemen, please, come in!"

He stood up and walked towards the visitors, who, complete strangers though – at least for the time being, were together with him under the same roof, belonged to the same household.

"Can I help you?" he asked those who had come to help.

"Our patient is safe and sound asleep," said the older carer.

It was obvious that he wanted to apologize for the disturbance, and what could have been more suitable for the purpose than to point out that the patient, the head of the family, was under the circumstances fine and sleeping peacefully and thereby underline that they, his carers, had done their utmost to achieve that.

"I thank you for the effort, gentlemen. Can I be of any help to you?" asked Blasius in the friendliest tone possible, for he wanted to show that he was well aware of what they had done and still were doing for his father.

"It is still too early to go to bed," said the younger carer at a low voice, shyly, almost apologizing, "and we thought..."

"Oh yes, certainly," Blasius interrupted him obligingly. "I usually go to bed quite late, at around ten o'clock; sometimes it's well past midnight before I turn in. It always depends on what I do: certain things keep me awake, others make me sleepy. Please come in."

"What you say is very interesting. The same thing is the case with us, although we can go to bed a lot earlier now than we were able to five or six years ago."

"Why do you stay up so long? Does it have to do with the nature of your work?" asked Blasius curiously, because it hadn't escaped his attention that in the past the two men must have had a different rhythm of life.

Before his visitors were able to answer his question, he noticed that they were still standing and asked them to take a seat in order to prevent them from having the impression that he wanted to get rid of them as soon as possible. They gratefully accepted his offer and sat down. It was obvious that they were happy. When Blasius offered them a cup of tea, they were delighted.

Now they were sitting comfortably on chairs arranged in a triangle facing each other and having a chat.

"Have you been working as carers long?" Blasius wanted to know.

A conversation was necessary, for it was obvious that the two men were seeking one, and what was more suitable to start with than a question about their occupation?

Personal experiences attach themselves to an occupation, and what are experiences if not an account of one's personal past? One believes they know somebody if one knows their past.

Blasius did not mean to interrogate his visitors, but somehow he had to start a conversation.

"How long have we been in the service of the cloister as carers?" the older carer asked his colleague.

"For about five years," answered the younger man.

After his brief answer there was a short pause which seemed to contain something unspoken.

Something must have happened five years before that had induced both men to take up the occupation of carers. Now they belonged to a tiny minority, for indeed very few people were willing to work as carers in the service of a cloister. Therefore the carers' journey through life must have been an unusual one.

"Did your previous activity have anything to do with nursing? How did it happen that you started attending to sick people? Is it not an occupation which requires the study of anatomy and lots of other things?"

Blasius was now quite curious and asked several questions, expecting his visitors to tell him more about their past. The older carer understood that he was supposed to give detailed answers to Blasius' questions and he was willing to do that.

With his body leaning forward and his hands between his knees, he emanated a sort of repentance. That was at least the impression he made. His colleague remained silent; however, his look was not directed to the floor but to Blasius.

"Our," started the older carer, pointing briefly to his colleague, "journey through life has been very strange."

The way the carer began his story made Blasius believe that his supposition was right and he wanted to learn more about that strange journey.

"May I know more about it?" he asked and it was obvious that he was genuinely interested in their life story.

"What we are going to tell you is very personal but we both have the need to impart it to you," the carer said, and raised his head. Now he was using his hands a lot while he was speaking. The young host's sincere interest in their life story encouraged him to go into detail. He and his younger colleague had the need to tell the story of their past lives to someone of high intellectual standing, someone who would be able to understand and therefore not to scorn them.

"My colleague is quite a bit younger than myself," began the older carer. "Before we decided to become carers, we used to be highwaymen, the worst criminals."

Due to Blasius' earnest, mild expression and gestures showing his deep interest in the story, the narrator felt encouraged to continue and open up to his listener.

"Please tell me more about it," said Blasius.

"At the very beginning I was alone," the older carer continued. "I attacked rich travellers, threatened them with firearms and robbed them. And if someone tried to make use of his firearm against me, I just killed them."

The carer told his story with a completely neutral expression. There was no remorse in his voice, although his body made an entirely different impression. No other emotion could be gathered from what he said either. Blasius had the feeling that the carer was able to speak calmly because he reported on a time with which he had nothing to do any longer.

"That means you killed people?" asked Blasius to be sure that he had understood the carer's words correctly, for what he had heard was not a usual life story, no usual biography. In front of him was sitting a man who during his earlier life used to rob and kill people and who did it consciously and on purpose.

"Several of them," answered the carer shortly and unmistakeably.

"And what was after that?" asked Blasius, for he wanted to hear how the crazy story would go on. There was, in fact, no point in enquiring further about the murders, because now he knew that the man in front of him used to be a highwayman, whose hands were stained with human blood several times.

"After a certain time it became more and more difficult to work alone," said the carer.

"Why?" asked Blasius, extremely interested to know every detail.

The narrator for his part was ready to answer any question and hide nothing; he was ready to confess.

"People would no longer travel alone," he continued with his story, "but rather several together in groups. Threatening and robbing them all at the same time became almost impossible. At that time I thought of giving up. However, my colleague joined me."

Here he turned to his companion, who confirmed what had just been said with a slight nod and a corresponding gesture.

"He himself had also been working alone before that and struggled with the same difficulties. Therefore he also had thought of giving up. It was a lot easier to do the job together. Now we were an inseparable, dangerous duo. Business flourished!"

"And why did you decide to abandon it?" Blasius interrupted him, because obviously something crucial must have happened, something that determined a new direction for the two now devotedly working men – a turning point in their lives.

Blasius was more interested in turning points than in anything else. In his opinion each turning point was a new birth, the beginning of a new life and of a new world.

"I think my colleague can answer your question better than I," said Rusus, the older carer, turning to his younger friend.

"One day there was a Jesuit amongst the travellers, a small, unobtrusive man," began Orlando. "He gave us all he had, including his address and urged us to visit him, telling us he had something special, a surprise, for us. We never visited him."

Blasius listened to his guests impatiently. His whole body was trembling, because he could hardly wait for the end of the story, although it was already known to him: the two men were now carers, his guests. The end was the present moment, which contained all that the two men and he himself had ever experienced. And finally, in that same present moment converged everything that the two carers, he himself, all known and unknown people had ever met and would ever meet – all their past and all their future.

"Please go on, please," he urged Orlando to continue with his riveting story.

"We fleeced the travellers thoroughly, sent them on their way, stuffed the loot into bags and disappeared."

"And then?" asked Blasius, almost anxious that his guests might stop telling their story.

"Soon we reached a place known only to us. No other person would have had any reason to go there. That was our hiding place. There we were safe and did not have to fear anybody or anything from outside. However, human life isn't just determined from the outside, but also equally from the inside, where there seems to exist a point of contact with the eternal. There, sluice-gates of eternity open in due course to let the eternal flow into practical life. When that happens, a new person emerges and at the same time the former dies. The new being knows about the former one, however no longer personally, because the turning point lies between the two. Therefore the two are alien to each other."

A short pause followed. Blasius needed it, for the last words of the younger revealed that his guest was acquainted with the significance of the turning point through his own experience, something that was and had to be reserved only for the few.

"Then I noticed that something had happened inside me, a sort of conversion," continued Orlando. "I felt a need to lead a completely different life. When I told my colleague," he said pointing to Rusus, the older carer, "what had happened in my innermost being, he just looked heavenwards and thanked God with all his heart for the immeasurable grace. And true grace it was indeed, by no means deserved, a pure gift. Only then he turned to me and told me he felt the same. We immediately went to our hiding place, where we had left all we had looted, the money and all the precious objects made of gold, jewels and pearls, put it in bags and the same day took everything to the abbess of an orphanage. We were in disguise so that she could not see our faces. What we have told you, sir, nobody else has ever heard. You are the first to know it. You can accuse us and our death is certain, or you can choose to protect us. We are in your hands."

The narrator stopped speaking.

Blasius asked no more questions, because everything was clear: before him, under his father's roof, there were two people who had committed multiple murders and who, if judged by the law in force, should have been executed without any ifs and buts. At the same time, they had experienced a sort of conversion, a change so deep that now they were dedicating their lives to serve those in need.

Acting strictly in accordance with the law in force would

have required that they be reported to the authorities and punished like any other citizen would have been punished for a similar deed. Now they were, however, new people who thought and lived in a completely different way. Punishing them for their previous deeds would have been to do them wrong, because in that case the sentence would have been passed with the intention to punish those highwaymen, however they did not exist any more, they had been dead for five years. The punishment would have hit those who cared for sick people and expected no remuneration.

Such were Blasius' thoughts. He turned sideways and stared at the milky panes of one of the windows. No clear picture emerged in them.

He was silent.

"Moses experienced conversion and so did Saint Paul and Constantine and Augustine and these carers also, and undoubtedly many others besides. I have not yet been granted the privilege. What am I doing wrong?" he asked himself silently. There was deathly silence in the room.

"Did you knock on my door with the intention of telling me your life story?" he asked his guests.

"Sir," replied the older carer, "our personal conversion story is our most valuable possession, the most precious thing we know. We wouldn't like to possess something that could appear to us holier and more precious, for what we already have grants us everlasting happiness. For our work as carers, we do not expect any remuneration; we are doing it out of gratitude to God for rescuing us from the claws of evil and to be of service to our fellow beings."

"I haven't yet been allowed to experience this sublime feeling of gratitude," Blasius thought during another short break.

"At the time of our conversion I was forty-one," added the younger carer, "and my colleague here was six years older. We are happy it didn't happen later or we wouldn't have had much time left to lead a different life."

"But are you here just to tell me this?" Blasius inquired again.

"No, sir, we decided to tell you everything in order to ease our hearts. We are grave sinners, who found grace before our Lord Jesus who led us onto the right path. We haven't deserved it; we have deserved to be burnt in the infernal fire. But lo, Jesus has looked after us. We wanted to tell you about our happiness. All of us Jansenists have had a similar experience, a conversion, and it's this experience which unites us. Because this deep conversion is the single inexhaustible source of bliss, we should like to share our happiness with others."

"Is access to your circle possible for everyone?" asked Blasius, for in that moment he desired to join the Jansenists' circle, who so readily shared their happiness with everyone.

"Possible? Oh sir, it is the greatest joy for our small circle to welcome a new member. That is the case at our headquarters in Paris, in our branch here in Rouen and wherever there are Jansenists."

"I am deeply grateful to you for this information," said Blasius, obviously very happy with the answer.

"It is getting late," he said pointing at the clock on his desk.

"Now I should like to suggest that we go to bed and have a rest. Tomorrow, we could perhaps visit your community's house here in Rouen. I can hardly wait for it.

Good night, gentlemen."

Both carers seemed thrilled with the suggestion, because they were convinced of having won a new member – an extraordinary one.

"We shall have a quick look at our patient to make sure that he is sleeping comfortably and then we will go to sleep, too. Good night, sir."

The carers left the room and silently closed the door behind them.

The unexpected visit was over.

*

Just a short while before their visit Blasius had known nothing about the two men, but now he knew more about them than anyone else. Before their visit, Jansen and Jansenism were merely words, which he was not able to associate with any certain content; now, however, he knew two people whose lives had been determined by Jansen's ideas and whose story had made such a strong impact on him that he himself was considering the idea of joining the Jansenist movement.

***

Apart from a few twinges in the right side of his abdomen, Blasius had almost no discomforts during the night. He slept well and felt refreshed the next morning. He had no difficulty getting up, though he usually had severe backache and it always took him a while to straighten up. All that made his father's carers appear even more pleasant in his eyes. He attributed the reason for his own unusual well-being to them.

After the carers had bathed and fed their patient and made sure he was comfortable, they went, accompanied by Blasius, to the Jansenist Society house, which was about ten minutes' walk away.

In the garden of the Society's house they met Mr Guillebert, a lean gentleman of about fifty years of age. He was in habit of rising for a short morning-prayer very early every day and after a frugal breakfast, which followed immediately, he spent the best part of his time in the garden. He received both carers and the unexpected guest in a friendly manner and proudly showed them his fruit trees, his bees and his freshly set vines.

Blasius did not praise all he was shown out of mere politeness, but because he was truly fascinated by it.

The entire garden radiated an extraordinary calmness; the only sound that could be heard was the twitter of birds. Mr Guillebert tried to make his guest aware of many things by pointing at them.

The monastery was a magnificent stone building, a castle with thick walls and numerous turrets. The castle owner, an elderly nobleman without offspring, who felt attracted to the Jansenist doctrine, had put it at the disposal of the Jansenist Society.

The garden was separated from the wide area which surrounded the castle by neatly trimmed hedges, granting the entire estate a character of noble seclusion.

Through a gap in the hedges, the small group left the garden and went into the parkland which also belonged to the estate. Magnificent trees, some over a hundred years old, stood towering their majestic tops towards the sky.

*

Blasius had never been in such an estate before. He felt overwhelmed by the mightiness of the trees and kept looking up most of the time, marvelling at their high tops. Not accustomed to long walks, he felt quite tired after only half an hour and suggested a short rest to his companions. The two carers and Mr Guillebert were slightly embarrassed that they had not thought of that before and immediately hastened to fulfil their guest's wish. They proceeded at once towards some inviting benches that stood nearby facing each other in a corner with ornamental shrubbery.

Blasius was glad to be able to rest a little. Only after he had sat down, he noticed how tired he was, because his legs felt like lead.

"You said you recognized only and exclusively the teachings of Bajus and Jansen, if I understood you correctly," Blasius continued the conversation.

"That's right," replied the older carer.

"Our leader, Mr Guillebert, also appreciates Calvin very much," he continued, pointing to Mr Guillebert, who in return smiled a sort of approval. He knew that pointing at him undoubtedly meant that they were talking about him, or that he was, at least partially, the topic of the conversation. He was completely deaf and he never spoke, which is the case with most deaf people, because they do not hear their own voice and cannot control it. As he could lip-read certain words he was busy all the time putting pieces together and trying to get the meaning of what people were saying. Silence was his only faithful companion; however, because the opposite was unknown to him, he did not know silence either. He gave all orders in the monastery in writing and by gestures. Although he never spoke to anybody his competence was indisputable.

This time he did not know the topic of the conversation, but he knew that it could only be religion. He did not need to worry that the two carers would not be able to explain everything in detail. Like all other Jansenists they were informed about the principles of the Jansenist teachings and could provide anyone who was interested with accurate information. In addition, their former life story made sure they spoke with unadulterated enthusiasm.

"And what about the Jesuits?" asked Blasius.

"What the Jesuits teach is not true," continued the older carer.

"Could you explain your view a little? I would be very grateful for that," asked Blasius, indicating with a corresponding hand movement that the question was directed to all three of them.

"The Scripture teaches us," began one of the carers in a didactic tone, "that man sinned, gravely sinned, right at the beginning of his earthly existence, which was in the Garden of Eden, because he ignored the will of God, and that everything that happened later was a direct result of this first, original sin. Therefore, this sin is inherited from generation to generation. It is a true original sin, something we have inherited from our parents and that we must pass on to our descendants."

"I understand that," Blasius said quietly, "but how does this sin manifest itself in our practical life?"

"This sin determines our whole life, down to the smallest detail," continued the carer, "nothing of what we think, feel, do is exempt. Even our best intentions are nothing but sin."

"But that is only the diagnosis of the disease from which we suffer," Blasius said quietly, "but what can you do about it? Could you suggest a treatment?"

"You can't do anything," the carer answered. "It is not a usual sin, which can be repented, atoned for or resisted." The carer's voice sounded drumming, prophetic.

"And you really can do nothing about it?" Blasius asked; he was disappointed.

"Only one thing can be done, and that is to recommend oneself to God. God alone in his wisdom has forever decided whether he will or whether he will not exercise his grace some day. Man should neither demand nor claim nor expect anything."

Blasius listened carefully, because what he had just heard was completely new to him. What he had known before was that sincere prayer and sincere repentance opened all doors and were heard by God with unlimited certainty.

"Can man at least hope?" he asked the carer.

"He can, but that won't in the least increase his chance of success."

"Not in the least?" Blasius wanted to make sure.

"That's right, sir, not in the least!"

"Not even if the person is sincerely trying to do good, to help his fellow men, when he prays and follows the rules in the Scripture?" asked Blasius, because he could not easily get used to the idea.

"Not even then," replied the carer decidedly, his implacable face resembling that of a statue. "For all human endeavours," he continued, "are without any meaning and can under no circumstances affect the predetermined divine order."

"I am a mathematician," said Blasius, calmly justifying, "a friend of precision and clarity, and therefore I would like to ask a clarifying question."

"A clarifying question is always welcome, because what we represent and teach does not tolerate ambiguity."

"If the divine decision is predetermined, fixed forever and if it therefore cannot be influenced in the least by human activity – otherwise it would not be predetermined –then even evil deeds can have no effect on divine providence?"

"That's exactly it," replied the carer decidedly, although the content of the question should have set him thinking.

"Then it is – in terms of efficacy – exactly the same whether one seeks to do good deeds or commits crimes?" Blasius added.

It seemed as if the carer had hesitated to reply for a moment, because Blasius' question had touched on something that the Jansenists and indeed all other supporters of the doctrine of predestination had never thought of. The question clearly demonstrated that predestination offered no incentive for people to do good deeds; it moreover absolved them from all responsibilities, seeing that all the best efforts could have no influence on God's eternal decisions.

Although the break the carer needed was very short, it seemed to last much longer, because the visitor's delicate question demanded a particularly clever answer. It couldn't call predestination into question, yet it had to convince the interlocutor's astute logic.

"We're not saying that it is the same," the carer continued, somewhat embarrassed, "but merely that human actions cannot influence God's eternal decisions."

The feigned relaxed attitude of the carer could not obscure the fact that he was dissatisfied with his own answer. For though good deeds and bad deeds were different things, they had no effect on those of God's decrees which related to punishment and reward in the hereafter, and thus, according to religious teaching, to the meaning of human life and salvation. If that were true, however, all that man did was superfluous; man himself was redundant.

In that brief pause the carer desperately sought a satisfactory answer, for such considerations crept over his heart, and the same thing happened to his colleague.

Their deaf leader neither heard nor understood anything nor did he notice that something unexpected had happened. Though he didn't miss the slightly anxious expression of the two carers, he attributed it to their fatigue. He didn't have even the faintest idea that he had just lost two devoted members. Even less could he imagine that the loss had been caused by a single perspicacious question asked by their guest. The two carers were from that moment on only formally members of the monastery, for their thoughts were elsewhere. Blasius' last question had shown them clearly that the whole doctrine of predestination was untenable.

The guest himself, whose fascination with the impressive life story of the two carers had led him to the Jansenist movement, couldn't have guessed what he had caused with his specific question.

He in turn had received an answer from the carers, the character of which was to him as a mathematician not unknown. A strange spark had flown between pure mathematical logic and the pure irrationality of religion: good deeds and bad deeds were not exactly the same, however, their achievement was the same, because they did not achieve anything, at least where it was crucial – before God. So there they were the same, although they were different; a paradox. That there was something similar in mathematics, he could still understand. Although mathematics required clarity and precision, paradox was not alien to it. He had those numbers in mind of which it was said they could never follow one another, as there were between any two of them an infinite number of other numbers of the same kind; therefore they were infinitely many everywhere. And then he remembered that embarrassing question: which number is greater, all those numbers together, or only those numbers of the same kind that can be found between any two such numbers? He had spent many a sleepless night mulling that question over, and now it appeared there, where he had never expected it – during the conversation about the immutability of divine decisions.

An abysmal relationship appeared to exist between those two worlds, because the number of single elements in the universe of such numbers had to be infinite, but also the number of single elements between any two members within this universe was an equal other universe, the same size as that, although only part of it.

The infinite number of elements between any two elements in the universe of such numbers was only an infinitesimal part of the whole universe, so logically speaking it had to be smaller, infinitely smaller, than the whole universe. But that was not the case; the part was equally powerful as the whole, neither bigger nor smaller, but equal. He rejected the idea that of these two infinities one was larger than the other, although many a mathematician thought that way. He even went so far as to think that those who claimed such a thing did not understand the meaning of infinity.

Therefore they had to be equally powerful, although the mind had difficulties accepting that.

However, they were not identical, which was also the case with good and bad deeds.

The carer's answer had made a strong impression on Blasius, no less strong than the one his well-aimed question had made on the two men. It had revealed to him a totally unexpected aspect of human life that was completely unknown to him before. It was the aspect that so-called good and so-called bad deeds were always the same, although they had fundamentally different contents, as well as that human activity was indispensable, although – in absolute terms – it could not achieve anything.

This thought was not a completely new visitor to his mind though; however, he could not easily accept it and grant it a permanent right of residence in his mind.

"Either they do not understand me, or I do not understand them," he thought to himself and did not move. The three men before him did not stir either; each of them did not do it for his own reasons.

For a while there was complete silence; that was the only thing they had in common in that moment.

"How do you know that everything is just like that?" asked Blasius and continued without waiting for an answer. "For, if even man with his prayers and good deeds cannot get through and have any effect on divine decisions but has to wait outside for God's mercy, from where can he then claim to have the knowledge of God's highly personal matters and intentions?"

He felt that the question he had just asked required a good answer, because it was about something extremely interesting, the possibility of fundamental knowledge, which was always valid.

"It is clearly written in the Scripture that one's own life cannot be extended even by a single second. There is no justification for this," answered one of the carers.

It was neither an explanation nor an answer to Blasius' question.

The Jansenists allowed themselves to assert in the manner of the Holy Scriptures whatever they wanted without being obliged to justify their assertions. Once the assertion was made it received its body and its life and it could be defended easily and hardly thought of as dispensable. Blasius felt that nothing could be achieved by asking more questions.

He couldn't imagine, of course, that the two carers had nothing more to say, because their previous religious belief had suddenly vanished. The only things they could still offer as evidence were ready biblical claims that required no logical proof.

"And why are you against the Jesuits?" he asked the carers, trying to steer the conversation in another direction.

"Our views are fundamentally different from theirs," said one of the carers.

"In what way?" asked Blasius.

"The Jesuits claim that man has free will and can act freely, therefore do willingly good or evil and thereby earn eternal bliss or eternal damnation. The greater the intellectual abilities of the individual, they say, the greater the responsibility that he has before God. In their opinion every person deserves his salvation or his doom.

We abhor the idea that man can deserve his bliss or his damnation. The Jesuits think that man is a partner of God and therefore has the right to say something and to participate in making decisions.

For us, the individual is merely a subject of God, and God alone is the Lord."

"I understand: in the opinion of the Jansenists man has no free will," Blasius said, to clarify and to hear more about it.

He himself had given the matter much thought countless times and examined all the possibilities according to the strict mathematical logic but he had never found a satisfactory answer. That's why he had asked to hear if those strange men would come up with an unexpected idea.

"That's correct," replied one of the carers vigorously, "everything is predestined up to the last detail, to the end of time. Free will is an invention of the godless infidels."

The carer spoke very clearly and very loudly, while looking heavenward in transfiguration so that the whites of his eyeballs were visible from below. He spoke as if he implored God to cast the worst curse upon all who thought differently, especially the Jesuits.

Mr Guillebert smiled with satisfaction, because the rapt look of one of his members meant that he was teaching the erring the eternal truth. He could not have guessed that this expression was not one of ecstasy but merely a direct consequence of a habit. Blasius thought the carer's expression was strange.

"If that is so," he said firmly, in order to lower the ecstatic carer back to earth, "then the human way of thinking itself is predestined, all human characteristics, abilities, inclinations, the human way of experiencing and evaluating things..?"

Blasius expected the carer to become insecure after having been asked such a question. But nothing happened. The latter lowered his head a little, looked Blasius into the eyes and said calmly: "That's exactly it!"

"But then the original sin of our first parents in Paradise has been predestined by God and therefore our own failures, too?"

Blasius had hardly uttered the last words, as the carer looked at his pocket-watch and said loudly, almost shouting: "The patient! We must return immediately!"

The two carers jumped up and ran away.

Blasius sat a while with Mr Guillebert. They looked at each other; however, they could not talk to each other. Then they stood up and walked back to the monastery building. There Blasius said goodbye to his host, with whom he hadn't exchanged one single word, and walked home at an easy pace. On his way home he did not meet anybody nor was he disturbed by anyone.

"Did the carers really rush home because of my father or did they not have an answer to my last question? Or did they want to gain time in order to think about it more carefully, because the question is not an easy one?" Blasius thought.

"One of these must be true. So far nobody has found a satisfactory answer to the last question I asked the carers. I have thought about it many times, but I am still as in the dark about it as I was at the beginning."

***

A few weeks after his accident, Etienne Pascal felt comfortable. At night he could sleep well, and the pain in his broken leg had almost ceased.

One evening he asked Louise to call Jacqueline and Blasius, because he had to discuss something with them.

Louise had no difficulty finding them: Jacqueline was sitting in her room writing a long poem that she wanted to dedicate to Mother Angelique, the head of the Port-Royal monastery. She was surprised when Louise told her that her father wanted to speak to her. There was something official and serious in the invitation to her father's room through the maid. Never before had she had a conversation with her father that was preceded by such an invitation. Although one could justify the invitation through the servant by the fact that her father could not move without pain yet and had no choice but to have her sent to his room, she felt, however, that her father wanted to tell her something special.

No sooner had Louise called her than she laid the pen down, closed the inkwell and went to her father.

When Louise told Blasius that his father wished to speak to him, he was sitting at his desk working on the improved model of his first calculating machine. He himself had intended to go to his father a few minutes later and see how he was doing. Now he was asked to go to him. Therefore he felt the invitation to be urgent.

He put his pen down immediately and hurried to his father's room. Jacqueline had arrived there just a moment before and had not sat down yet. They both came closer to their father's desk and stopped just a step away in front of it.

"How are you, Father?" Blasius asked in order to drive away the uncomfortable tension that had arisen in the room.

"Did you sleep well last night?" asked Jacqueline before Etienne Pascal was able to answer his son's question.

"Thank you, dear children, thank you for everything. I slept well and feel as good as you can in my situation. I am glad that you're here to give me the strength to persevere, and I'm also glad that I had two carers. They are capable people and they have done their job well."

"Do you need something, father, can we be of any help to you?" asked Jacqueline, although she felt that her father didn't want to speak to them about his condition or about the carers.

"No, dear children, I have everything I need, the two carers have thought of everything. I just wanted to talk a little to you, strictly speaking, to you, dear Jacquie, but it is good that Blasius is here, too; three are smarter than two, so it will be easier to find a solution. Sit down for a moment, so that we can talk quietly to each other. It is in my opinion about something important, perhaps crucial."

Blasius and Jacqueline brought two chairs and sat down.

"Dear Jacquie," began Etienne Pascal in a calm fatherly voice, "I thoroughly respect your decision to enter the Port-Royal monastery and to renounce the world, but I would like to ask you to postpone the execution of it for a year."

She was sitting demurely before her father in her long dress, which covered her ankles. Her delicate hands rested in her lap, pressed together between her knees, outlined through the dress.

"Why should I, dear father, postpone the enjoyment of

the highest happiness for a whole year? Please try to believe me that all other things this world can offer cause nothing but pain to me."

Blasius sat quietly and listened to the conversation. He did not know what the meaning of it was. Only one thing was certain: his father thought it was very important to dissuade Jacqueline from her sudden decision.

"I have just one single wish," said Etienne Pascal, as quietly and gently as before, "take enough time to think about everything before you make this step. Such a step clearly requires a certain degree of maturity in life, and you're still so young, much too young in my opinion. In short, I would like to spare you every disappointment, nothing else."

"I know about your love and your care, dear father," Jacqueline replied calmly and convincingly, "but I've thought it over thoroughly and I am mentally completely prepared to devote my life to God and serve him alone. Under the leadership of Mere Angelique, I cannot stray from the right path. I think I will turn in now, it's getting late."

Blasius knew his sister well and understood exactly what she meant by her last words.

"Dearest Jacquie, I told you my opinion, but I will take heed of your free will and your decision. Your happiness, dear children, is more important to me than anything in this world," said Etienne Pascal in a calm voice, however, a hint of sadness, disappointment and even bitterness in his words could hardly be missed.

Blasius had noticed everything.

"Now I will have to return to my work, I should like to finish it before going to bed; besides, I feel extremely tired and not well at all," said Etienne Pascal as if trying to apologize.

"The effects of the bone fracture have not improved; on the contrary, I feel them more and more every day, every hour so to speak. But now I feel an uncomfortable pressure in my chest, a particular one, I cannot breathe," said Etienne Pascal, panting heavily.

"Shouldn't we send for doctors or at least good carers?" Blasius asked anxiously, although he felt that his question was not suitable, because his father's suffering could hardly be alleviated by medical skill.

"No, dear Blasius, my suffering has now taken on a form that cannot be cured by any doctor. But now I must send you away, my work is waiting."

Her father's last words were exactly what Jacqueline wanted to hear, because she was waiting for a suitable moment to withdraw.

"I wish good night to both of you," she said and left the room.

Blasius stayed a short while alone with his father, because he felt that he needed to clear up certain things with his father before it was too late.

"Just one more moment please, dear father," Blasius turned to Etienne Pascal, who was about to arrange the documents on his desk according to content and urgency.

"I am listening, dear Blasius, what is on your mind?" asked Etienne Pascal, and he put the papers he had been holding on the desk and turned his tired face to Blasius. His dull eyes were surrounded by large dark circles and deep sunken in their sockets.

Blasius knew that his father kept no secrets from him, because there was something that drew them to each other and joined them together. It was something that required the most precise distinction and separation, and at the same time permitted the boldest and most original links, as life itself does. That something was mathematics, the art so abstract that it was based on nothing, but at the same time capable of being as concrete and specific as desired to relate to almost everything. He also knew that those who were familiar with the strange art of numbers – a tiny minority by the way – tended to believe that they were the chosen ones. But he also knew that those chosen few usually had a melancholy trait, for what made them special could relate to almost everything in life, but not to everything, and what their art could not relate to seemed to be the crucial ingredient – the spice of life.

"I have the impression, dear Father, that you have special reasons against Jacqueline's decision. Am I right?" he asked his father.

"Yes and no, it depends how you look at it," replied Etienne Pascal.

"What do you mean?" Blasius asked.

"I am not against it, because my opinion is that each person should be free to decide about such things. And yet I am against her decision, because she is too young to be able to judge clearly. I hope you understand what I want to say."

"Yes, I understand, Father, I understand it perfectly."

"But that is not everything," added Etienne Pascal.

"What else is there to say?" Blasius asked curiously.

"Approving or disapproving of something has a somewhat rational, legal character; however, there is something which exceeds the rational sphere of life, and that is what saddens me," Etienne Pascal spoke slowly, his gaze focused on something non-existent, his right hand stroking his left as if it had been the hand of a beloved person.

"And what is it, father, which makes you sad? Please tell me, if I may know," Blasius asked.

"I loved your dear mother infinitely and felt her love for me every moment of our brief life together, and through you, our children, I continue loving her infinitely."

Blasius saw that his father's eyes filled with tears and that he was dumbfounded by what was happening in his inmost soul.

He stood up, approached his father and took his hand; the skin was pale, almost transparent, the blue veins were visible, and the back of the hand was covered with numerous light brown spots.

"Please tell me everything, Father, please," begged Blasius.

"My joy would be boundless," continued Etienne Pascal, "if Jacqueline and you had the courage to find life partners and put children into the world and thus enable that to continue living which gives sense and meaning to everything, because without a body there is no brain, and without brain there is nothing: no thoughts, no imagination, no ideas, either of..."

Etienne Pascal let go of his son's hand and made a dismissive gesture.

"Oh, let it be, one should not say everything; one should feel the most delicate things personally and not wait for them to be explained. Once they are uttered, their core gets divulged, betrayed," said Etienne Pascal, hardly audibly.

For a moment both of them were silent.

"But, dear father, if Jacqueline doesn't feel the urge, the desire to put children into the world, then you must try to understand her attitude. Let her go her way."

Etienne Pascal looked at his son with an air of someone deeply offended. Blasius was almost frightened. His father had never had that expression before. Suddenly there was something hostile in his parent's usually mild face. His eyes sparkled while he was wiping the tears from his cheeks.

"I have already done it," he said resolutely and with a touch of warning. "You needn't play her lawyer. She told me everything clearly herself. I understood the meaning of her words well. The scent of the candles in the monastery and the voice of an old abbess are obviously more attractive to her than the smile of a child. If that is so, then any conversation about it is superfluous."

Blasius noticed that his father had changed thoroughly. Never before had he spoken about such things. The world always seemed to be in order, even when there were a thousand wounds in its body. But now everything turned out to be lies and deception.

"But, dear father, it's not her fault, it's neither her will nor her desire, but it is the eternal predestination, invariable, constant and unalterable."

Blasius spoke in the confident, convincing, relaxed manner of an experienced Jansenist missionary.

"What a wonderful world you are telling me about!" said Etienne Pascal in a trembling voice full of bitterness. "Who taught you that nonsense? Was Calvin your teacher? Or was it some other would-be-sage?"

He didn't expect any reaction from his son, because he did not expect anything more. Everything he could have been offered at that moment was worthless. He turned away from Blasius and muttered to himself, unconcerned about whether anyone was listening or not, because he had no one.

"What has become of my children! Good heavens, why have you punished me so?"

Blasius was standing so close to him that their bodies were almost touching each other. He understood that his father mentioned heavens and then punishment.

"These are higher insights, dear father, the only one capable of paving the way to perfect happiness."

Etienne Pascal didn't move. His son's words inflicted new pains upon him. All he wanted to say was no longer intended for anyone. He whispered words to himself, unaware of what he was doing.

"This is my end. Only now I realize that Fermat was not exaggerating when he once told me that even the best mathematician could be hopelessly stupid. At the time I could not agree with him. Now my own son has convinced me that Fermat was right."

He turned and looked at his skinny, pale son. His look contained a touch of contempt and disgust.

"Such insights lead to perfect happiness, you say?"

"Yes, Father, that's it," Blasius said quietly; his voice had overtones of strange calmness that resembled the calmness of a dazed person who, due to his daze, feels safe and on the right path.

"Then I may assume that you are completely happy now? I wish you more luck, dear Blasius, and a lot more insight because it seems that you are lacking much of it. That insight of yours, which you describe as high, doesn't seem particularly high to me."

Etienne Pascal's embittered, trembling voice had no effect. Blasius seemed to have taken a final stance, which in turn was more important to him than the happiness of his beloved father.

"All I say, dear Father, may appear ridiculous and silly to you," he said quietly and confidently, as intelligent and cultured religious people speak, "but only if one assumes that everything is predetermined and that the eternal divine plan can't be changed by anything, only then all things get their true value, and the smallest bit attains its dignity, for then the smallest and the largest become something unconditional in this world."

What Blasius had said sounded well thought-out, self-contained and convincing. There was no doubt that he had carefully considered and refined with his sharp mathematical logic everything he had heard from his father's carers. Now he provided indisputable statements, for every dispute required a logical approach. Here this approach wasn't possible, because everything that Blasius said was well underpinned and logically bolstered.

Etienne Pascal knew that well and therefore he was looking for a crack in the wall of logic in order to penetrate into the strange newly built world of his son and to loosen it, if possible, from the inside.

"But, dear child, don't you see that such a view doesn't only narrow man's scope but virtually abolishes it? The highest living being that can think, feel, plan and dream turns into a simple lump of matter that has nothing to say, a tyrant's toy."

Etienne Pascal apparently tried to wake in his young son a sense of pride and win him over to the idea that human dignity is at the very top of the value scale and that it must not be second to anything.

Blasius however knew that opinion, for already by the age of ten he had often thought about that and come to the conclusion that the greatness of man was contained in the capability of being aware of the human nothingness. Therefore, he was prepared to reply to his father's remark.

"But, Father, why do I need any scope, when I have been assigned my permanent place in the eternal working thanks to unalterable divine predestination? Thus I need not care about anything, because eternity provides for everything and for ever."

*

The man in Blasius had come to the conclusion that the conception of the human being as a striving noble creature that is supposed to be the architect of its own destiny should be abandoned.

Was that a relapse into medieval times of hoods and darkness, or was it the dawning of a new way of thinking completely incomprehensible to the ordinary mind, which followed after logic had played all its cards?

Again, it seemed that Etienne Pascal had found a weak spot in his son's well presented, calm, imperturbable arguments, a possible loophole that promised to allow access.

"But doesn't such an attitude smell of shrugging off every responsibility, discarding that which distinguishes man alone?"

He used these words hoping to touch that trait in his son's character which was abundantly available, which, however, now stood in the service of something that demanded everything, although it needed nothing.

"It is a decline," continued Etienne Pascal, "a relapse into the bestial, even the purely material, a rejection of consciousness, of the essence of our being! Don't you realize that, dear child?"

Etienne Pascal had to realize with disappointment that the promising back door was closed. Inside, there was a strange angel holding the bolt of the firmly locked door.

"We cannot provide for ourselves, dear father, nor can we get rid of that sin which clings to us all since the beginning of creation; only Jesus Christ, our saviour, can do it; he alone can do it, he alone does it and he alone will do it until the day of the Last Judgement. Then the final decision will be made: woe to those who have not prepared themselves, who are not girded with the cincture of certainty."

All of Etienne Pascal's good intentions, all his attempts to win his son for the cause of man, were in vain. He had nothing left in his hand that might have enticed him; no bait seemed to be good enough.

"Child, you're young, and the world rests on the shoulders of the young, no matter if the departing old regard it as incomprehensible, impossible and even hopeless. I wish you a good night. There is still some work left for me to do, not very much though, but it has to be done."

"Good night, father," Blasius said quietly and without even the slightest hint of regret in his pale face. He turned around and left the room with slow steps.

***

Etienne Pascal was left alone in his room, alone in the truest sense of the word. No one was physically present in his room, and inside he felt that his beloved children, his pride and his joy, had drifted away from him, gone into a world entirely alien to him, the thought of which made him shudder.

Never before had he felt so lonely. When the mother of his children, his beloved Antoinette, died, a wound which would never heal completely opened in his heart. The devotion and the gentle nature of his children helped him bear the pain. His son's outstanding intellectual abilities nurtured in him the confidence that Blasius would one day hold the office of a royal minister and enjoy all the tremendous benefits that accompanied such a high position.

But now the children were gone, each of them in their own way.

Gilberte was already married, had a family and therefore little time for her already aged father.

Etienne Pascal had desired a different husband for his beautiful Gilberte; he was not delighted by her choice at all. But at least she had chosen the natural way and seemed to be happy in her marriage.

His younger daughter, Jacqueline, had decided to abandon a normal, natural life and spend the rest of her days in a convent.

And Blasius, his pride, seemed to have taken to a strange doctrine which deprived him of every will to live.

He hadn't expected that from his children, however that which he could never have been prepared for had happened.

Now he was sitting alone at the desk in his room and stared at the opposite wall. He saw nothing, for nothing appealed to his eyes, nothing caught his attention. His childhood, his youth, the study of mathematics, acting as President of the Tax Office of Clermont, the marriage, the birth of three children, the death of his beloved life companion, the time in Paris, the move to Rouen, the growth of his children, and now the loss of those lovely children, whose thriving gave meaning and strength to his own life, everything was gone at once and now it was just a hazy memory of something he had perhaps only dreamed.

That he himself was still there he had no doubt, because he was considering everything and cogitating; and wasn't that sufficient proof that he was still there? He didn't like Descartes, because he found him too radical, however he couldn't ignore his most radical idea, for what else could be more convincing proof of existence than thinking?

Countless times he had tried to find an error, a weak point in the original assertion, but any attempt to argue against Descartes' statement was nothing but the best proof that the clever Renatus was right.

So he knew with certainty that he was there, but was there anything else that was worth being there for?

Etienne Pascal was looking for it, and as soon as something presented itself as a sufficient cause to strive and struggle for, it was exposed by him as empty and lame and as such discarded. He was truly soliloquizing, because he did not know that he was doing it. Hardly perceptible movements of his lips and occasionally audible sounds were the only signs that he was still among the living.

"The fourth act of my drama is drawing to an end. The tower I have built is high indeed, because I always wanted to stand high and overlook everything, but now I must state with horror and dismay that the height itself only blurs my view.

The power of the Kingdom and the glory of the Crown were always the only meaning in my life and their prosperity my only gain.

In my son, I saw already the future finance minister whose counsel is highly appreciated by the Crown.

I saw my daughters married to men of his standing. I saw them blessed with plenty of vigorous young life, indulged in happiness and wealthy. I saw myself always surrounded by hordes of grandchildren, still strong and healthy."

He did not know exactly what he was saying, but he felt he heard something that rhymed. He did not want anything. The words, which he thought rather than spoke, came from an unknown somewhere and disappeared into an unknown somewhere. He cared neither about their origin nor about their destination, because they neither asked for nor ordered anything, and they themselves were at the same time the message they were carrying, the content of the world, always identical for all people, yet always different for each person.

Etienne Pascal was gasping for breath. His pale, lifeless hands rested without stirring on his emaciated thighs. His weary head was leaning back and resting on the upper soft edge of his armchair, almost hanging over it.

"I have always planned and calculated. Now it is the end of the voyage of my barge, and everything is so tangled and intertwined that I cannot untangle it.

I no longer hear the rhyme.

The distances between the final syllables are too big for me. My miserable mind is much too coarse, without any force; I can notice only dead blocks without any juice between.

I cannot expect anything more, because all that was bound to come for me has already come. But I am convinced that my son will think differently in the following acts, for his fourth act is yet to come.

Either his insight will get even higher, allowing him to view his present ideas as totally ridiculous, or he will fall much deeper into the abyss of nonsense, so that even his current attempts to speculate about God and Divinity will then appear to him to be a blasphemous impudence of reckless intellect.

Whatever may be the case, his present way of thinking will appear to him to be stupid.

If he continues thinking in his present manner, it will be curtains for him and for everything that belongs to him – then my existence will have been void of sense and meaning."

Etienne Pascal's head was performing hardly noticeable nodding movements full of bitterness.

"My coach has always been robust and my coachman loyal and well-behaved; I have never dared or sought the impossible.

His coach is weak and frail, but his coachman is impetuous and foolhardy. Therefore the journey that is awaiting him is incomparably more dangerous than mine has ever been.

He will, no doubt, dare the ultimate, and whatever springs from it will be my son's child."

Etienne Pascal shook his head and his eyes filled with tears.

"No, no, for me, it is too much, too heavy. The fourth act of my life has been overloaded, a struggle, a wrestling with the angel on the river, the ever-flowing one, which separates the no-more from the not-yet."

His pale right hand took a white handkerchief from his breast-pocket and wiped the tears from his eyes.

"Perhaps you will be more successful, my son; for me, this struggle is much too strenuous, I cannot wrestle any more. Now I limp, my hip has been injured in this strange struggle; I cannot even stand upright, let alone run.

Now I will finally allow myself the deep sleep, the only genuine one, which never has to cease, without any limitations or barriers, in which everything must be free, because the only thing lacking in it is obligation."

Etienne Pascal's arms slid down lifelessly. His head leaned against his left shoulder, and stayed there motionless, because his neck muscles had no more strength. Only a faint, barely perceptible twitch flitted over his face, then his body sank down into the chair, into that same comfortable hollow in which he had spent the most active hours of his ambitious life.

His fourth act was finished, the curtain had fallen.

*

The invisible listeners and viewers, who were allowed to attend his presentation, were satisfied with the performance and granted him a sincere, tempestuous applause of silence. They made haste without being aware of it, because it was necessary to set up the scene for the next and last act, so that everything may run just as it should and so that nothing is lacking in the world, neither the awful beauty nor the disgusting dignity.

***

Etienne Pascal's funeral took place only two days later. It was a common burial. Except for the few family members only two officials of the Ministry of Finance were present.

Etienne Pascal's two carers were not there. In Rouen, he had been their last patient. After he had recovered from his broken leg and could renounce their care, they left the city and decided neither to return to their former monastery nor to go to any other.

Jacqueline abided by her decision to enter the Port-Royal convent. Blasius hardly heard from her any more. She for her part did not care about the world outside the convent's walls, and her sick brother belonged to the world that she had renounced once and for all.

Blasius now lived with his sister Gilberte and her husband.

Gilberte took care of her brother and did for him what she could. What she did for him would have been enough even for a very fastidious person. However for Blasius it was not enough. His eating habits, his religious austerity, his ceaseless preaching of a morality that was unsuitable for the living, his total aversion to anything that did not meet his expectations burdened her with additional work she could hardly cope with.

The only thing that made her uncomfortable position still bearable was the fact that Blasius spent most of the time in his room and was seen only at mealtimes. Most of the time Blasius wrote, but no one knew what he wrote about, not even his sister.

By the age of fifteen, he had begun to suffer from terrible headaches. Later on the headache was joined by a hellish torment in his intestines.

Dozens of doctors had tried their healing arts on him, but nothing had helped.

For many years, life was nothing but a continuous martyrdom to him, and as he grew older, his already terrible situation deteriorated rapidly. He was constantly in torment and, being tormented, he tortured all those who lived with him.

He couldn't say anything against Gilberte's efforts and Louise's ability, but he still had the feeling that Gilberte was not entirely devoted to him. He did not care that his sister also had a family. Inside him, the sick plant of jealousy thrived, the growth of which couldn't even be kept within bounds by his sharp mind.

That was also the reason why he never forgave Jacqueline her decision to enter the convent. He regarded it as an act against his person, because he had expected her to stay at home and devote herself to him alone.

Jacqueline, however, was an extremely inept creature, incapable of taking up any kind of work so it would have been impossible for her to take care of him, had she stayed at home. It was rather the case that she would have had to be taken care of. Secretly, he knew that, but he reserved the right to blame her for it and to be bitter.

*

One evening he sat alone in his room and thought for the umpteenth time about the possibility of a life hereafter, after leaving the earthly existence. He remembered the conversation between his father and Jacqueline in which Etienne Pascal had tried to persuade his daughter kindly and gently to change her mind and not to enter a convent.

"Jacqueline didn't sway," he thought, "she has always loved me, I know. But not even her love for me, not my illness, my despair, nothing, absolutely nothing could change her mind. The smell of candles, the choral prayer, the image of the crucified Saviour, the dark silence of the convent rooms means much more to her than the desperate call of her brother, who is now totally dependent on others."

He thought so, and although he was no closer to Jacqueline than to Gilberte, he felt somehow hurt and betrayed.

He was left with no choice but to shake his head although he knew he had no reason for that.

"Well, it is all strange, very strange," he mused. "I cannot understand her decision. Had she stayed at home, she could have looked after her brother who is in need of help. That would have been an excellent opportunity for her to help someone in need, to follow in the Good Samaritan's footsteps." He remembered his father's efficient carers whose piety was so exemplary and whose devotion to caring for others was so great that their simple life could have held spellbound every contemplative person; for that was exactly what had happened to him. He couldn't have known that those two had gone off and away. He could know even less that his perspicacious questions had caused a new turning point in their life and that they had abandoned and stopped believing in all that which they had infected him with.

"And yet she would have more than enough time to go to mass, to pray and to fast."

That was the way he spoke to himself, although he thought he knew exactly why Jacqueline had chosen to spend her life in the calm of a cloister.

"Maybe I'm wrong," he continued with his thoughts, "but I cannot help thinking that her decision is not entirely selfless. Jacquie's claims that she wants to serve God and give up everything else seem to me a little suspicious. Do we have to serve God in a group, or wouldn't it be as good, if not even better, to serve him quietly and unobtrusively as an individual? But all those theologians and clergymen whose livelihood depends on the community never fail to point out that the sound of a group prayer is stronger and more likely to reach the ears of our Lord than the hardly audible whining of an individual.

I can well understand their position, but why does my sister need such a thing?

The only explanation I have is that she needs the company of other women with similar mental abilities as hers in order to chatter with them. Of course, I cannot offer her that type of chatter.

Looking at things that way, I see why Jacquie claims that she enjoys perfect happiness in the convent.

It is not easy, but her decision should also be respected. If she has the desire to serve God alone, then she has found the right thing. In the eyes of a God who fits her intellect, she has probably chosen the best way of life."

Such considerations opened his eyes and helped him realize how much Gilberte and her husband were doing for him and that he had nothing to reproach them with.

"It's nice of Gilberte and her husband that they are ready to cook for me and attend to my needs. I can never thank Gilberte enough. She has more understanding for me and probably for any sufferer, because she has chosen a natural way, she has a family and is therefore willing to be patient and devote herself to others. Jacquie has never experienced that and therefore tends to think of herself in the first place."

*

Such similar thoughts crossed Blasius' mind that night when something strange happened that shook him out of his thoughts and reminded him that so-called human reality contained much more than he suspected.

It was already quite late at night. The sky was overcast with thick clouds, and outside there was complete darkness, filled with perfect silence, which is quite typical of the November nights in that part of the world.

All three windows of his room were open. Outside, no lights could be seen nor voices heard and there wasn't even the slightest breath of wind.

It was all the more surprising that one of the three windows suddenly slammed shut.

The bang was so powerful that it made him start and stand petrified for a while.

Then he went to the window, opened it gingerly, looked out for a moment and then closed it gently again.

He was so stunned by the inexplicable slamming of the window that he did not feel his pain anymore and he also stopped thinking about Jacqueline and her decision.

His natural inclination to get to the bottom of all things, the scientist in him, was directly addressed by the incident.

"Strange," he said, "no breeze is stirring, and then the slamming. It is also peculiarly dark out there – it's never been so dark. It is not surprising, of course, because at this time of the year, the end of November, the nights are much longer, and the sky is mostly overcast, so that no starlight penetrates, and the moon is also very rarely to be seen.

And yet I have the feeling that this night is pregnant with meaning, a special one. The wise have always known that utter darkness is the mother of the brightest light as well as that the brightest light causes utter darkness, because it can blind. Yes, yes, the extremes meet by touching each other. They do not actually touch each other, but merely come so close that the spark, the messenger, can, in accordance with the circumstances, fly from one side to the other."

He walked slowly to his desk and sat down.

His gaze fell on the crucifix.

"When I look at this crucifix," he reflected, "with its long pieces, then I am reminded of Descartes and his system of coordinates.

He, who believes in God in a different way from all of us, seems to be the first to have discovered the meaning of the cross.

It is a strange thing. Behind the simple form, I anticipate unfathomed depth, the ultimate. I see many possible applications of it. A builder can use it for his purposes, as when he builds a roof. A sailor uses it when he wants to determine the exact location of his ship. To the mathematician it is of immense importance, because it makes it possible to represent dynamic processes as well as the relation between continually changing values in a very simple way, by means of static lines.

His invention has added a new storey to the edifice of

mathematics. It is possible that his system of coordinates represents the highest level of thinking, because it touches what can only be thought or perhaps even only felt."

*

Blasius paused, for all of a sudden questions of a completely different kind came up in his mind, although they also had to do with the cross.

"Why was Jesus crucified? Couldn't he be killed in a different way?

It can of course be a coincidence. It may be that the Roman authorities used crucifixion as the most common death penalty in their empire. The penalty was very suitable for discouraging potential agitators and enemies of the empire.

All that is possible and it needn't be of any particular significance, however, the fact is that the Saviour of the world wasn't executed by sword or spear, nor was he thrown into the arena before the wild beasts, but crucified.

The Roman authorities must have known of the dangers that lurk in all sorts of legends growing up around liberators and martyrs. It is therefore astonishing that they didn't choose a method of execution in which the body of the executed person doesn't remain intact so as to prevent any swindle and the birth of a legend.

They could have burnt the remains of the executed and scattered the ashes to the four winds so that there was no definite burial site – all such methods were known to the Romans. Why didn't they do that?

The Romans were not naive. They knew that legends build cities and states, but also destroy them.

No, no, no, there must be more to it!

The cross guards the inexhaustible mystery of the world, its beginning and its end, its entire coherence.

The higher one progresses in the knowledge, the deeper layers of the cross-dormant secrets one uncovers. The joy of knowledge grows with understanding, as does the insight that the amount of the unknown hasn't diminished, which is of no minor joy, for the unknown is the eternal source of longing and imagination; it keeps the mind alert and does not permit that the fountain of glory ever runs dry.

Descartes seems to have penetrated furthest into the mystery of the cross. He created the universal frame of reference after the form of the cross; or possibly the sign of the cross has always been the simplest and the most elegant expression of something universally valid, and he was just the first to recognize that?

It is conceivable, of course, that lots of other systems of reference can be created, but that does not alter the point. The idea of introducing a frame of reference is crucial.

If some day other systems of coordinates are to be invented, the meaning of the Cartesian system of coordinates will never diminish, for they all must be derived from his idea.

One way or another, he is the creator, because to realize what the essential is means to liberate it from the realm of meaninglessness. He is the liberator.

Is it at all possible for the mind to penetrate further in this direction? Hardly, because the system of coordinates offers a frame of reference for everything the mind has to deal with. Therefore the mind has no need to keep searching. It is saturated, and it cannot be more than saturated.

Any over-saturation would be no progress, but a relapse. Anything that goes beyond absolute saturation can't be digested and is rejected as a disgusting nonsense.

Then completely different laws are in force, those of the heart."

***

Blasius sighed with relief. A blissful smile shone from his face and lavishly filled the room. Something had happened inside him. The menacing darkness of the autumn night and the unexplained slamming of the window had triggered something in his mind, something which he otherwise would never have experienced. Now it was there and he had every reason to rejoice.

"That's what it is!" he said loudly.

"Somebody who, thanks to his brilliant mind, manages to create the system of coordinates, the universal frame of reference, cannot go any further, because he will feel satiated and won't have the slightest desire for other things.

All Descartes can do now is to die, and that will happen soon. Probably during some ridiculous, totally useless activity, because he cannot keep on going the way he did. He has followed only his mind all the time, however, now his mind is exhausted, because he has reached his zenith. His extraordinary mind will grant him the favour of some powerful people. At the same time it will undoubtedly provoke the envy of the grovelling entourage, and they will see to it that he disappears."

Blasius took the crucifix in his hand and turned it slowly and carefully, looked at it from all sides, as if asking it to tell its secret to him.

By doing that, he raised his head, as if seeking contact with heaven. His gaze fell on the calendar on the wall before him.

"Today it is the 23rd of November. There are still 32 days until the birth of the crucified Saviour. That means one entire lunar cycle and a seventh part of it. Exactly between the 24th and 25th day of the twelfth month the

Saviour comes into the world, which yearns for him and which infallibly rejects end even kills him in order to long for his new arrival even more ardently."

He shook his head. He had allowed himself to be led and entertained by his own thoughts and did not know where they would take him.

Now he arrived there, where everything looked different. Everything seemed to be a pure contradiction, and yet everything seemed to contain more truth than all the logic operations taken together.

"Can reason help there at all? Each year, the Saviour is born again, he suffers each year anew, each year he is crucified afresh, and each year he rises again. No state can be skipped, because each one brings forth the next. Thus, in each single state all others are contained, so thoroughly and completely that a single state, in fact, does not exist."

Blasius looked at the clock, that funny product of the human mind used to divide and measure something that in itself was neither divisible nor measurable and that stubbornly resisted any attempt of the mind to comprehend it, its own most terrific child.

"Soon it will be half past ten. Not a single lit window in the town can be seen. All candles are extinguished. My fellow citizens' weary limbs are resting. It's so dark outside that probably even the thieves and highwaymen are asleep in their hide-outs.

And I, weak, sick, a permanent abode of suffering and pain, am awake!

What for? What do I want? What am I waiting for?

My candle is already going out, it's only a few millimetres high, and then it will be dark in my room, too. I've always had pain, I am used to having it, as it were; I'd probably feel rather strange if I suddenly hadn't any. But what I feel and have to endure now can no longer be called pain, it is an infernal torment."

He sat down in the chair at his desk, leaning forward, and his sickly body automatically took up the position in which he remained whenever his pains were especially strong. Only the elbow of his left arm touched the surface of the writing desk, and his forehead leaned on the palm of his left hand. His right arm was resting lifeless on his right leg.

"I needn't read the story of Job to learn about extreme suffering. Just as the last drops of the melted wax disappear by being transformed into light so is my pain increasing. I no longer feel the usual pain in my body because what is now raging in my brain does not tolerate any other pain.

The candle flutters already, the wick is burnt, and the flame is suffocating in the last drop of that which is burning. The clock shows half past ten, the beginning of the night's core, of the three central hours, and my cup of pain is full. Not a single drop more of it can I bear."

***

Blasius could not see anything, because the candle on his desk had gone out. The darkness in his room and the darkness outside were now melted into one another. He could not see anything nor did the situation allow it, for no source of light was visible, and yet he suddenly saw something so bright that even the brightest day would have appeared dark in comparison with it. The vision was so overwhelming that he could not remain silent. He simply had to say it aloud, he had to impart it to someone, and he screamed as loud as he could. However, all happened so quietly and indistinctly that even someone in the immediate vicinity would not have been able to understand anything.

In the room filled with complete darkness only some faint noise could be heard, which must have been caused partly by irregular banging of arms and legs against the floor and the sides of the desk and partly by frightening, convulsive attempts to cry. Nothing could be seen, only heard.

It is not possible to say how long the noise lasted, but what significance can be attributed to time if all that happens consists of visions?

After a while, the dull thuds on the floor as well as the gnashing of teeth and the suppressed, convulsive cries stopped.

Immediately after the silence that followed, some distinctive words could suddenly be heard. They were spoken at a very low voice and sounded as if uttered by someone who – due to some indescribable miracle – had just been rescued from the jaws of a monster, which devours everyone and everything.

"Fire! Fire! Fire!" could be heard.

Any outsider might have thought a fire had broken out, although there was no sign of fire or flame.

The light seemed to be the predominant aspect of his fire vision.

The addressing words "Eternal God" followed. They did not sound so much like a request for help and assistance but had rather an undertone of triumph and satisfaction at knowing he was at last one of the chosen few to whom God had shown himself in his noblest appearance.

"God of Abraham, Isaac, Jacob! God of Jesus Christ!" followed immediately, the exact explanation as to who was meant by the 'eternal God'.

"Certainty! Your God is my God! Amen," the voice underlined the steadfastness of the vision at the end.

However, it remained unclear which of the mentioned biblical figures was meant by 'your'.

Was it Abraham, the first mentioned patriarch of the chosen people and the creator of the eternal, abstract and unimaginable God?

Was it Isaac, the blessed son of the first patriarch, whose conception occurred contrary to the logic of the usual human experience and who reportedly imparted a deeper meaning to the act of blessing?

Was it Jacob, the hidden aspect of the entire man?

Or was it the controversial offspring who on the one hand must have come – it is true, only after a purification process of three times fourteen generations – from the loins of the first patriarch and the creator of the true God; who on the other hand, however, was begotten in a non-carnal manner?

The words dissolved in the silence of the night and charged it with suggestions. After the vision, Blasius was exhausted and slept peacefully. A gap appeared in the heavy cloud cover, and a delicate, dim ray of light crept through the window in his room, but it was too weak and could not wake him.

***

Gilberte never woke him in the morning, for she knew that because of his severe headache he could not sleep at night and therefore often stayed in bed until noon.

That was the case this time, too. When he woke up, the day was well advanced. After the strange experience, the sleep was a sheer bliss to him, and he was as well as could be expected under the circumstances, for his pains had subsided a little. The vision was still so fresh in his memory, and he had the feeling that it was, in fact, an experience he had had in the waking state, that has always been a part of him.

And yet he knew that it was a unique experience, something very special.

Now he was aware that a new period of his life had begun. The vision was a sort of dividing line between his previous life and his new way of experiencing the world. Before the vision he had in mind the idea to write a detailed mathematical work, because he had believed that only mathematics was able to explain the fundamental connections and secrets of the world. Then he realized, however, that he couldn't understand the behaviour of his own father although both of them were good mathematicians and loved all that was logical.

After the vision, he abandoned the idea altogether.

Before the vision, he regarded religion as something that simply belonged to the human way of thinking; as something that was practiced in a particular manner, in different parts of the world and at different times for fear of unknown powers, personified and called gods. All in all, he had regarded it as a product of human fantasy, completely illogical, yet helpful to simple people; for those of great capacity for grasping abstract ideas however, completely unnecessary.

The only exception in that respect was for him the Christian religion, because he thought that all forms of religious feeling – including the religion of the Hebrews – which preceded Christianity had been a preparation for the Christian religious feeling as the highest one of all.

After the transfiguring vision in the darkest of nights, the Christian religion became for him the core of everything, the keeper of the meaning of life.

Because he had felt so overwhelmed by what he had seen he decided to write down on a sheet of paper what he must have spoken during the vision and sew it into the lining of his favourite coat.

Gilberte had already heard him rumbling in his room, but she did not want to disturb him, because she knew that he appreciated very much being left alone, if possible.

He for his part knew what she thought and did not need to fear that she might suddenly open the door and catch him sewing.

He took a needle and some thread from the drawer of his desk. With his penknife he cut open the seam of the lining, inserted the sheet of paper and sewed the lining up again. Then he stood up, holding the cloak in front of him and examining his own work.

"Not bad for someone who has never tried to sew before," he said to himself in a low voice.

"Whoever does not know that something is in there can't notice anything. From now on, I will wear this coat until my last breath. Its content is richer than the entire wisdom of the world.

Now I am also one of the few chosen mortals since Moses to whom the Eternal has appeared in the form of fire. I'm glad that the vision was in the form of fire, because the other forms do not seem to be of equal rank. Fire is doubtlessly the finest and noblest one of all and is closest to the eternal truth itself."

He put the needle and the rest of the thread back in the drawer; then he called Gilberte. He didn't have to call a second time because she appeared after a few moments. She knocked on the door before opening it – he insisted on it.

He answered her question as to whether he had slept well with a perfunctory "yes" and before she could put any further question to him he asked her not to never wash or mend his coat, under any circumstances.

"Why? I do not understand. Clothes must occasionally be washed or cleaned," Gilberte tried to understand the reason for his peculiar request.

"All right, all right," replied Blasius, visibly irritated, "I know, I know, but in this case that does not count!"

It was obvious that he didn't want to confide her some secret of his.

"But why not, dear Brother, it is still in good condition and won't disintegrate if it is cleaned or washed. That must be done, because sweat and dirt…"

Blasius interrupted her. He knew all her logical reasoning, but he did not need it because he had other, more cogent reasons for not doing it.

"Berti love, let's not waste any more words. Your arguments are well known to me. You are probably right but in spite of all, do as I tell you, and the matter is settled. Is that clear?"

Gilberte shrugged the affair off.

"As you wish," she said, "Less work for me! Get ready, the confessor you have sent for will be here any minute."

"Oh yes, you're right, I almost forgot, it's good that you reminded me."

He went to the wardrobe and took out of it some clothes he intended to put on.

While leaving the room Gilberte tried to think of a reason why her brother had such preposterous wishes.

"He probably has hidden something in his coat, something that must not get wet. It must be some sort of document," she thought, although she could not imagine what kind of documents he might have hidden.

"I will find it out, it must come to light. Only what becomes known must have been hidden once."

Then she suddenly remembered that she had to hurry, because Father Anselme – that was the confessor's name – was probably already there, waiting for someone to open the door.

She shouted to Blasius, urging him to hurry up; then she ran downstairs.

"All right, all right, I'm ready," he replied in a calm voice in response to her cries.

Only a few moments after he had heard her steps quickly follow each other on the creaking stairs, he heard her talking to someone and slowly ascending the stairs.

"Father Anselme seems to be here already," he said in a low voice to himself. "The Jesuits seem to be punctual in unimportant things; I wish they were as accurate when it comes to the crucial issues. The confession is something crucial, I'm curious to know how he'll confess me. He doesn't suspect that I have invited him out of sheer curiosity, but mainly because I still need more suitable material for the next *Lettre*.

I've already confessed to a Dominican, to a Benedictine, and now I want to confess to a Jesuit, one of those I consider to be faithless.

I've always appreciated punctuality; what a pity that a Jesuit is in possession of such a noble virtue.

But why am I doing all this? Just out of pure curiosity, or do I want to clarify something? I am not quite sure. Am I not mocking at the sacrament that I revere infinitely?

Father Anselme would never have come himself; I have sent for him. Jesuits do not offer themselves, they only come when they are invited; that seems to be generally known, in my case that is true. I alone am responsible for everything that should result from this visit."

While he was soliloquizing, Father Anselme and Gilberte entered the room.

"Brother, I am bringing along someone to you," said Gilberte with a smile and introduced the invited father confessor, an elderly, small, thin man with fine regular features and a merry twinkle in his eyes, to her frail, pale brother.

Upon entering the room Father Anselme doffed his hat, walked over to Blasius and shook his pale outstretched hand.

Father Anselme greeted his host with a simple "Laudetur". He spoke with extraordinary ease, but without even the slightest hint of routine. He bowed a little, which granted his greeting a special touch of grace and decency.

"Semper Laudetur," Blasius replied amiably.

"Welcome, Father, take a seat, please."

Father Anselme thanked him and sat down in one of two chairs standing against the wall, after he had gathered his black cassock at the front with a spontaneous, skilful movement. Everything he did must have been studied carefully and on purpose sometime in the past, however, now it was part of his personality. It was obvious that he always did it in the same fixed manner, because he simply could not do it differently.

*

"Thank you, Mr. Pascal. I am pleased to be able to visit you. Above all, I am glad that you want to confess, because in life it is of paramount importance to be able to confess."

Father Anselme stressed the words 'to be able to' so strongly that it could not be overlooked.

Blasius listened attentively to his guest. He had often thought about confessing but never discussed it with a confessor. Now the confessor he had personally ordered unintentionally made confession the topic of conversation just a second after he had sat down.

Blasius found his guest's wording peculiar, because the core of Father Anselme's assertion was 'to be able to'. That made Blasius even more curious and enhanced his wish to hear more about it.

"Why do you think, Father, that the confession is crucial in life?" Blasius asked, for he was very eager to hear the Jesuits' point of view. Never before had he spoken to any of them.

"Because by means of confession people are given the opportunity to answer the question 'Where are you, Adam?'

in all honesty, without fear of being punished with the loss of Paradise. On the contrary: the opportunity opens the doors that were firmly closed before man; it shows him that he is not hated, that despite everything he has the right to enjoy life, whoever he may be.

But we must never forget that there is only a sincere confession. An insincere confession is a pure negation of itself; it is an additional bolt on the already locked gate that leads to peace."

"Do you think, Father, that confession to oneself is also valid?"

"It is not only valid; it is actually the only valid way, without which everything else is worthless. It is the highest form of confession, the only honest one; however, there always lurks the danger of being insincere. Insincerity itself destroys the soul and splits the person. That happens in such a subtle manner that someone who confesses to himself seeks to convince himself that he is acting correctly, takes his own part and thereby turns against himself.

Confessing to somebody whom one trusts is more sincere, because two people listen to what is being said."

Never before had Blasius heard such an explanation and he would never have expected it from a Jesuit. He was trying to find some juicy elements of hypocrisy in Father Anselme's words; he had invited him with the intention of getting some suitable material he needed to render his next *Lettre* even more biting and offensive than the previous ones; however, he could not find any.

"It is an honour for me, Father, to speak to you," Blasius said. His voice sounded sincere. "May I offer you a glass of wine?"

"Only if you take one, too," replied Father Anselme quietly.

His reply was somewhat diplomatic.

"I mustn't, unfortunately, my doctors have strictly prohibited it," Blasius apologised.

"Then I won't have any either. I should not like to drink, eat or live alone."

Father Anselme had mentioned three things he wanted to share with other people, and each of them demanded an explanation.

What he meant exactly Blasius didn't know but he was so impressed by his guest's words so that he spontaneously said: "Wonderful!"

"By refusing a glass of wine you have given me a whole attitude to life, of course, in its basic features. It seems to be a superb one, and I would like to learn more about it."

Blasius wanted with all his heart and soul to have a conversation with someone who was obviously not a usual interlocutor.

"I am at your disposal, Mr. Pascal," said Father Anselme, and a peculiar smile crossed his face, a smile that can only come from perfect composure when it is coupled with the ability to marvel also at something unimportant and banal.

"What are you trying to emphasize when you say that you would not like to drink, eat or live alone?"

"I should not like to drink alone from the river of time, because it would mean to let all others die of thirst. Then I would die of loneliness of the heart, and undoubtedly no one would be an exception in this respect.

Let us remember, Mr Pascal: the eternal produces the transient in order not to feel lonely.

Everyone who during this short journey chases away the loneliness maintains the eternal, his own home, works on it."

What Father Anselme had just offered as an explanation sounded good, even very good, but it was for Blasius no less enigmatic than what was supposed to be explained. And yet he relished every word in the Father's strange response.

"And why not eat alone?" asked Blasius eager to hear more.

"To eat alone would mean to absorb the world alone – that would not be a feast."

"What is a feast for you, Father?"

"A feast is always the joy derived from the joy of others, the unification of separate pleasures. It is the joy of travelling through the world. The journey, however, requires a landscape. The landscape itself is always structured and playful, never alone, never a single undivided thing. It is always the other side, the world as the second person, which we can address and only thereby become what we are."

Blasius enjoyed the words of his guest, but he felt that he would enjoy their content even more if he understood it better. It seemed – to him at least – still too impenetrable, incomprehensible. Therefore, he interrupted Father Anselme.

"Could you please explain more precisely what you mean, Father?"

"The journey creates the person who makes it, it creates its creator; thus he is at the same time completely free as well as totally dependent."

The words of the guest were generous and awoke his desire to hear more. Blasius liked each of Father Anselme's supplements more than the previous one, and yet each time he felt he had not understood the most delicate part.

"Now I understand even less," he thought to himself.

"Who determines the direction of our journey, Father?" he asked his guest.

"You see, Mr Pascal, people ask such questions as long as they think in the usual temporally-religious manner."

Blasius could not believe his ears. Before him sat a clergyman, a confessor, someone who was generally regarded as a representative of a religion which showed hardly any interest in change and compromise; that same clergyman described the religious way of thinking as usual and temporally, by which he obviously meant inferior. He had never thought such a thing possible nor heard of anything similar.

"Why do you associate temporality with religion, Father?" he asked, because he wanted to get to the bottom of it, for he saw no direct connection between religion and temporality.

"They needn't be associated with each other," Father Anselme said quietly, "because they are closely related to each other; they are two different variations of the same thing. By the way, religion is not a Christian invention. Since the moment when man became aware of himself, which means since the beginning of the world, man has always been both religious and non-religious; self-awareness implies both. The so-called ancient peoples had crowds of all sorts of deities, to whom they sacrificed and on whom they felt dependent. They also had the idea that everything that happens was controlled and determined up to the tiniest detail by supernatural external powers and that everything, without exception, was bound to happen just as those external powers decided. Some went so far as to allocate in the predetermination of the world exact roles to special deities, so that some of them decided about the duration of everything, that is the theoretically quantitative aspect; others carried out strictly defined measurements and thus made the purely theoretical become perceptible; and still others put the fixed arrangement into practice. Seen that way, man has nothing to say, because his life is – like all other things – predestined up to the smallest detail. This view of life is still not only alive but even predominant.

However, there have always been – albeit very few – people who did not believe in any predetermination by external supernatural powers. There are such people nowadays, too, and such people will always exist."

"And what are your views on this, Father?" Blasius interrupted his guest, because he felt that the moment had come to find out how members of the Society of Jesus really understood predetermination.

"Don't you feel that God knows everything down to the tiniest and most insignificant trifle in advance? And because God is omniscient," he asked another question, which was supposed to make the previous, rather neutral one appear a little clearer and more to the point, "for him all things must have happened in advance, before the foundation of the world, that is before they become part of the human experience, mustn't they?"

Father Anselme did not try to interrupt him, because he felt that Blasius, because of his own insecurity, had the need to speak a lot and loudly to stifle the tender feeling that all he had thought was right might be wrong, after all. He had asked two questions one after another, but they sounded more like statements, which demanded nothing less than an unrestricted agreement.

"The fact that for God everything is already done, before the beginning of the world, is crucial, Father, isn't it?" Blasius continued.

"The fact that God knows everything in advance and that for God everything has been done in advance, shouldn't be called temporal, should it? Man in his narrow-mindedness cannot, of course, understand that, can he?"

It was not clear whether he had no more questions or whether he himself had noticed how strange it was to ask further questions without having received any answer to the former ones, but Blasius suddenly stopped.

The silence that followed did not last long, but it seemed much more charged, because just a second before the room had been filled with Blasius' loud, shrill voice.

Father Anselme took the sudden interruption as a sign that he could start with the explanation.

"Well, Mr Pascal, things seem to be slightly different."

Blasius listened attentively and tried not to interrupt him.

"As long as one uses words like 'in advance', one thinks in temporal terms," said Father Anselme.

Blasius' gaze rested on the Father's calm face and he had the impression that he personally had already been changed by his guest's first words. Without blinking, he was all ears. However, he could not understand why people were thinking temporarily as soon as they were using words like 'in advance'.

"Could there be a completely different way of thinking than mine and yet be also correct?" he thought.

"Would you say that God is not omniscient, Father?" he asked Father Anselme the same question again to create a suitable platform for the defence of his world view and at the same time to learn what his guest's opinion was.

"Actually there is neither in advance nor afterwards, and what we in space and time call our reality, this transient world of ours, is but our way of experiencing eternity," said Father Anselme.

Blasius found Father Anselme's words strange, because how could one imagine anything without a chronological order?

"Do you mean to say, Father, that God did not create the world as omniscient and that he therefore needn't know everything in advance?"

"I would never deny that nor would I assert that it is so," replied Father Anselme quietly, "for whence can I take the liberty of judging what God knows and what he does not know? Is it not a blasphemy to ascribe to God all kinds of properties by claiming that God has the knowledge of something, can do something, is like this or like that? Are such speculations not impudent attempts to design and shape God's nature, to force him into a particular form and decide what he should be like?"

Never before had Blasius heard anything similar nor had he thought about it. It would be exaggerated to say that Blasius' personal world view was shaken by Father Anselme's words, for he felt safe in his temple of his personal religious ideas. However, he experienced them as a challenge.

His guest's words asked him to give up the security, integrity and finality of his own world temple, which he had unintentionally built around himself – in the manner all organisms do it – from the material of his entire personal life experience, and which grants every conscious creature the feeling of existence.

He felt the need to hear more about the Father's views and ask him more questions about this and that, not least in order to feel confirmed and safer than before in his unshakeable faith, by views that differed from his and thereby proved to him that he was on the right track

"Do you mean to say, Father, that, despite all the wonderful signs and proof as well as the announcements of the prophets that the Holy Scripture tells us about, we cannot know anything and therefore should not make any assertions about God?" he insisted further.

"I do not deny that the Holy Scripture offers an abundance of splendour, probably much more than we all together can say, however, it imparts to each reader everything in a language that only he and nobody else can understand. Thus each individual gets his own portion, his own *manna* as it were, during his way through the desert of his practical existence. Only what each individual feels is what matters. Every attempt to describe or to illustrate it to others is inevitably a false step, because every description avails of defining words and limiting pictures. For that reason every attempt to describe or characterise God is inevitably a defining and confining one and therefore useless, because it cramps and confines."

"What do you mean, Father?" said Blasius with irritation in his voice.

"On the other hand, if you declare God unapproachable," continued Father Anselme calmly, as if he hadn't heard Blasius' nervous question, "you declare God something that neither mind nor intellect can grasp, that therefore must inevitably remain beyond the human sphere. That means that man cannot have anything to do with God. In that case you build an insurmountable wall between God and man."

Blasius stared at the small, thin man in front of him, because he could not understand how someone could talk about such important things in such a calm and self-confident manner as if he were intimately acquainted with all he was speaking about. He asked no clarifying question.

"In either case," said Father Anselme, "God becomes a miserable piece of research by theologians who ascribe all kinds of properties to their guinea pig, receive thereby doctorates and titles, become famous, enjoy a comfortable lifestyle and through their actions cause confusion in the lives of their fellowmen; that confusion is sometimes so grave that they kill each other in the name of God's love; quite often the confusion is so skilfully done that those poor fellows are even grateful to them for everything.

These are ultimately the results of the two attempts to define God." He pronounced the word 'define' in such a way that he stressed 'fine'.

Blasius was silent and stared at the floor, but saw nothing, for he listened with his whole being to the guest, and what Father Anselme was speaking about led away from the visible.

"Define, Mr Pascal," continued Father Anselme, "means – as you know – to fix limits, to delimit."

Here Blasius lifted his head as if suddenly startled awake by someone.

Father Anselme's last words contained something strange. On the one hand it could be understood as an amusing, though not particularly serious wordplay; on the other hand a very common, much used word seemed to have a very deep hidden meaning, which people hardly ever thought about.

He felt that Father Anselme's words were all of a sudden heading for a realm entirely unknown to him. He didn't say anything because he was afraid he might interrupt the thrilling journey.

"Whatever is defined is limited, just a splinter, Mr Pascal," continued Father Anselme.

"Splinter of what?" interrupted Blasius.

The brevity of his question clearly showed that he had listened to his interlocutor very carefully.

"It is always but a single voice, a sliver of silence. Only silence is the source of all voices, all splinters. If you hear any voice, you cannot hear the silence. If you manage to hear all voices at once, you hear the silence, the unity hidden in the colourful attire of the multitude. One of the central ideas of the Holy Scriptures of the Hebrews urges everyone to listen to the unity of all voices, because they all make up the *unity of all forces*, which creates the world and which they call *Elohim*. Only he who in the deafening noise of the world can hear the unity of all voices becomes a conscious creator of the world, a complete human being, Abraham, the father of the multitude, under whose roof each single element finds its proper place."

"But we have learnt of God through the Holy Scripture, from all the events with Abraham, Isaac, Jacob, from the words of the prophets and the words of that one who was announced by the prophets centuries before his incarnation," said Blasius trying to speak confidently and with superiority, because he was aware that he was referring to something that was equally regarded by his guest as well as by himself as indisputable truth.

"You, Father, and I, we all have received the good news in the Gospels! Can we simply deny that?"

"That has been repeated indefatigably for many, many centuries, and lots of people had to die after cruel tortures, because they had dared to call something of it into question, or just to point cautiously to some contradictions in the whole structure. And yet the whole matter seems pretty unclear."

"What's unclear?" asked Blasius, as if afraid that something could still remain unclear to him.

"Many refer to the God of Abraham, Isaac and Jacob and to whom, according to the Holy Scripture, Jesus also refers. They all refer to him, however, in many different ways and with many different intentions, so that they are able to kill each other in the name of God. That is happening now in some neighbouring countries. There, the rulers determine what should be the proper faith for their subjects. Is that not a terrible misunderstanding?"

"But whose voice did Abraham, Isaac and Jacob hear, and to whom did Jesus pray in the hours of despair in the garden of Gethsemane, shortly before his death, while his disciples were sleeping?"

Blasius' questions still contained much of his previous confidence, and yet it was obvious that he was asking for an explanation.

"Your question, Mr Pascal, should be put to Abraham, Isaac, Jacob and, of course, to Jesus. They could perhaps give a satisfactory answer. I personally should not like to play the role of a lawyer who speaks in their name and answers such important questions, for which he cannot be appointed. That would be indeed the worst form of arrogance."

"But Father, they cannot be asked any such questions."

"And why should that be impossible, Mr Pascal?" asked Father Anselme in a calm voice.

"Abraham, Isaac and Jacob are dead!" Blasius said with surprise, because he could not understand how someone with education and thorough knowledge of the Holy Scripture could make such unreasonable remarks. Spiritualism was anyhow on the list of the practices strictly forbidden by the holy Christian church. He waved his hand in a manner that expressed his disappointment with Father Anselme's inability to comprehend such a thing.

He himself as a mathematician did not believe that the living could communicate with the dead.

"Indeed?" said Father Anselme, pretending not to have noticed Blasius' gesture.

"Certainly they are dead; it is written clearly and unmistakably in the Holy Scripture that they all died and were buried."

"And Jesus?" asked Father Anselme, almost impish, and a delicate slightly ironic smile sparkled in his gentle eyes.

"Jesus is not dead," said Blasius, "but he cannot be asked such questions!"

"But try, Mr Pascal, to give me a single reasonable justification for your claim."

"Jesus cannot answer this question," Blasius said with some hesitation, like someone stepping gropingly forward in the dark. His voice sounded a little confused, because he felt that his answer could not possibly convince – he himself did not like it either. However, nothing better came to his mind. In the short break in which he was waiting for Father Anselme's next remark, he had the feeling of having said something very clumsy and stupid. Nothing had been further from his thoughts than describing his Saviour in the way he had just done. The misery into which he saw himself fall now seemed to him to be immeasurable, and a better, redemptive response, by which his now questionable Redeemer should again be true, unequivocal, absolute, omnipotent, didn't come to his mind.

Where could it come from, if the one who was the source of all that was essential couldn't answer one of the most important questions?

"He *cannot* answer it?" Father Anselme asked, stressing the part of the question which had caused Blasius' misery.

"No, I did not intend to say that," said Blasius, without a moment's hesitation, desperately trying to reject those previous words and their sinister content as soon as possible, but they remained hanging in the air: he had denied his Saviour omnipotence.

His entire intention was so completely focused on how to correct his blunder that any other answer seemed to him to be more acceptable than the one he had first given. Therefore, he did not notice the snare contained in his new assertion, which he uttered to correct and clarify his earlier statement.

"He does not want to answer it?" was his new assertion.

No sooner had he said it, however, than he realized that he would never have intended that or should have said so. That answer was not appropriate for the nature of his Saviour either, for the objective and the meaning of the doctrine of Christ had to be to grant people eternal life. And was there a better way to achieve that than to tell them, clearly and unequivocally, to whom they should appeal in order to attain eternal life? And what was the meaning and raison d'être of that one who, in every respect, was the very core of holy Christian teaching, if he was not able to or did not want to tell people who the only true God was, from whom mortals could hope to be given eternal life?

"He does not want to do it?" was the next questioning remark of Father Anselme's, whose mind seemed to be, despite his advanced age, very alert, and who listened carefully and asked carefully directed questions.

"How do you know, Mr Pascal, that he cannot or does not want to do that?" he added another question.

Blasius' already very pale face seemed to have been drained of its last drop of blood, because he had no reasonable answer to Father Anselme's last question.

He rubbed his sweaty brow with a trembling hand, as if trying to help his brain find a better explanation.

"I'm experiencing once more that persistent headache that affects me each time I have to think hard," he said, asking almost imploringly for indulgence.

"We cannot know why he cannot or will not answer," he added, hoping to lead the whole thing to a tolerable end by changing the question.

"The question was not about whether he cannot or whether he does not want to," was Father Anselme's next uncompromising remark, "but how can you, Mr Pascal, assert that he cannot or that he does not want to."

"I cannot answer your question," Blasius replied immediately, because he felt that he could not change the direction of the question or give a satisfactory explanation for his own assertion.

"I believe you, Mr. Pascal, and it shows once again that religions thrive precisely where the mind is incapable of offering a satisfactory explanation, namely in troubled and murky waters. One can fish there very successfully, because there one can assert anything without taking any responsibility. There nothing is supposed to rhyme or to make sense. On the contrary, the stranger it sounds the better. Indeed, Mr Pascal, religion draws its life force from the absurd.

However, once there is a neat explanation of a mystery, religion vanishes from the now comprehensible, familiar sphere – it moves into the still unknown. Therefore, the most ardent defenders and advocates of religions are those lacking insight, that is, who do not know the explanation. When they defend their religion, they defend their own living space, their stamping ground, no different from all other living creatures."

Blasius listened and said nothing.

"Those who know a clear answer to such questions, a satisfactory explanation," continued Father Anselme, "do not need any religion."

"Is it conceivable, Father, that some day people will be able to answer all questions like these satisfactorily and that thereby the religions will disappear?" Blasius asked his guest, like a little child asking an adult for an explanation. He was glad that he did not have to answer Father Anselme's questions any more.

"That time needn't come, because since time immemorial, since man became aware of his human nature, he has, in fact, known the answer to such questions. The difficulty arises from the fact that the vast majority of the world population, which is after all responsible for the general feeling in the world, is completely ignorant of it. The very few have always known it, the very few know it today, and that will most likely be the case in the future. If most people knew the real state of affairs, there would be no guessing, no conjectures, no irresponsible assertions concerning God, heaven and the afterlife, no religious formalities and rituals, in short, no religions, each and every one of which tirelessly inculcates into the heads of its members the idea of being the only one in possession of the real truth, therefore better than the others."

"Do you want to say that the holy Christian doctrine, which shows people the only safe way to salvation, is but guessing and making conjectures?" asked Blasius, this time a little more confident than before.

"What it shows to them, Mr Pascal, I do not know," replied Father Anselme calmly, "however, the path on which its supporters tread seems to me to lead anywhere except to salvation. The most ardent among them serve their God so zealously that they are ready to stamp out all others who think differently; it is a very strange state of salvation. We in the Society of Jesus are not very enthusiastic about such practices."

"But it is the members of the Society of Jesus who are, more than anybody else, being reproached for their using all means to achieve their ends," Blasius interrupted him, glad to have discovered a weak point to launch an attack.

"All of us in the Society of Jesus are well acquainted with that sort of criticism; however, our enemies do not know that all that is but a big misunderstanding."

Blasius wished ardently to hear more about the victory

of that widespread accusation of the Society of Jesus and why it was a sheer misunderstanding.

Father Anselme on his part wanted to fulfil his host's wish, but at the same time to seize the opportunity to impart the real state of affairs to probably most capable person among the opponents of the Society of Jesus.

Blasius could not even dream of the possibility that in the Society of Jesus he was considered as a possible, in fact, the most probable author of *Lettres à un provincial*, in which the Society of Jesus was strongly criticized in extremely elegant language as a criminal organisation. Due to its witty descriptions, but not least because of the superficiality and ignorance of the readers, those writings were the most coveted read among those who considered themselves the intellectual elite, and offered an inexhaustible source of entertainment in the salons.

"All of us in the Society of Jesus," Father Anselme continued, "devote ourselves to high goals, probably more than anybody else; however, we consider our goals only if their realisation does not contradict our supreme principle.

This supreme principle of ours is based on an insight which is in our opinion the most fundamental one. Without that insight, all human actions are in fact a monstrous nonsense, regardless of whether they are something completely trivial like chasing a fly out of the room or removing a piece of a thread from the coat, or whether it is a so-called great deed like the foundation of a town or the creation of a new state. The greater and the more important a deed seems to be the more monstrous and senseless it is in our opinion if it is not in harmony with that fundamental insight."

Father Anselme's words had made Blasius curious and he was eager to learn about that fundamental insight without which any deed – regardless of how big and important it seemed to be – was inevitably senseless.

He thought that such an insight was something in itself not possible.

"And what is that fundamental insight you have been speaking about, Father?" he asked.

"That cannot be explained to people who are still thinking in a temporally-religious way."

Father Anselme's words erected a barrier which to be overcome required a completely different way of thinking; that way of thinking seemed to be rarer than anything else in the world.

Blasius had the feeling of standing in front of a closed door, of being forced to stay outside, of being excluded – in spite of his outstanding mathematical knowledge, in spite of his religious zeal, in spite of his intelligence; that hurt him deeply.

"Tell me again, please, what you meant by temporally-religious; I still feel that I do not understand it yet," Blasius asked his guest in a friendly manner.

"As long as someone thinks," continued Father Anselme in a friendly tone, "that once in the past there was a Noah who survived the Flood, an Abraham who discovered the true God, an Isaac who – contrary to the usual human experience – was born to very old parents, a Jacob who cheated his father and stole the blessing, a Moses who received God's law on a mountain peak, and a Jesus who by means of his death redeemed the entire mankind etc. etc., that person cannot live and act for the greater glory of the eternal. Therefore, whatever he does is pure nonsense. If that which he does is a small deed, it is a small nonsense, if it is a great deed, it is a great one. Such a person could never belong to the Society of Jesus, even if Ignatius had appointed him his successor, because the organization's formalities have nothing to do with the essence of the matter."

"You, Father, speak of living and being active for the ever greater glory of the eternal," Blasius interrupted, "but what are the works of man worth? All human activity is but a squirming and writhing of a miserable worm."

Thus spoke Blasius and his expression betrayed his deep disgust for that perceptible, mucous something that we mean when we use the general and indefinite word 'life'.

"The feeling of contempt for human actions, Mr. Pascal," said Father Anselme softly and slowly, "is the precursor of misanthropy, because human actions are perceptible and tangible signs of that which occurs inside the human being. All disparaging remarks about the life of man as the bearer of so-called original sin help to justify the destruction of his body for some so-called higher purposes. Then – so it is said – only something bad is destroyed – the worthless scum of the earth, for example. Am I right, Mr. Pascal?"

Blasius felt thunderstruck by Father Anselme's last words. He had the feeling that Father Anselme had pronounced the words 'worthless scum' with emphasis.

Suddenly, he remembered the events in connection with the protests of the poor in Rouen in which his late father had played a not particularly honourable role. He could not help thinking that Father Anselme knew of the attitude and the role of Etienne Pascal.

After a brief pause, which reinforced Blasius' conjecture, Father Anselme continued.

"Nothing is easier than to declare man a sinful creature. The consequences of such a declaration are, however, grave. The most powerful religions speak, for example, tirelessly about the inherent sinfulness of human beings as the source of all human torments and sufferings. And because people are fundamentally sinful and bad, they should claim neither liberty nor the same rights, because all the pain and suffering they have to endure are ultimately the consequence of their wickedness and their disobedience to God.

That is the religious way of thinking, which no doubt ensures, more than anything else, that things run just as they do. Due to this way of thinking nobody is supposed to have any conscience or feeling of responsibility."

"But the Christian religion teaches us that all men are equal before God, and calls on the rich to give to the poor; you know that, Father," Blasius said in a didactic voice.

"Of course, all religions urge the rich to give to the poor," said Father Anselme, "but by doing that they imply that some should always be rich and some should always be poor; thus the rich should always have the opportunity to do good deeds. Those who consider all sorts of donations made by the rich never think of the true nature of such donations."

Blasius was silent.

"Every current injustice," continued Father Anselme in the same tone, "an ever so cruel exploitation of one person by another is shamelessly justified as a deserved punishment for old mistakes, made a long, long time ago when everyone suffering now was in the state of his ancestors. Therefore, no suffering follower of a religion has the right to expect an improvement of his situation during his lifetime. Sacrifice and fasting, although compulsory, are no guarantee that some day in this life poverty and misery will cease. All religions promise their members eternal happiness in the hereafter. During this life they should neither claim nor expect anything. Everyone may, however, hope to enjoy a better life after his death. Yes, Mr Pascal, the generations sink hoping and expecting on the sharp edge of the time-abyss.

In particular those same religions that preach very diligently and persistently the sinful nature of man do also deny that man has any free will, claiming that he was created by his God as he is and so everything he did was ultimately the will of his Creator.

Who is then responsible for the stupid behaviour of man? Is it the Creator who has made man the way he wanted to and who must have known that his creation would fail, or is it man who could not even have a say in the creation of his being? How many people think about it?"

"But the members of the Society of Jesus, dear Father," Blasius interrupted his guest, convinced he had found a weak point, "claim that man has free will and at the same time they forgive all sinners all the sins committed. Is this not a contradiction, dear Father? For why should man sin if he has a mind and free will and can distinguish good from evil, and as such must be aware of the consequences of his actions?"

"Just because man can have free will, it is also said that he can sin. Without the possibility of one's own free will the sin itself is not conceivable. He who lacks free will cannot know what he does and is free from every sin, like an animal," said Father Anselme.

"The misery of man does not arise from the fact that he has or has not his own will, but from the fact that his own will – which is practically always present – is very rarely accompanied by insight into the unity of the world. The misconception lies in the fact that almost all people in the world confuse man's own will with man's free will.

Someone without insight cannot have free will, although that person's own will may be very strong.

Those who act without insight act like animals and therefore they are innocent. People whose actions are guided by insight can make blunders, however, never sin, because they cannot possibly have evil intentions, and that is crucial, the only thing that counts. It can often be heard that someone has done something terrible with criminal intent, knowing exactly what he was doing and should therefore be punished severely. Such claims arise from the same ignorance as the cruel deed in question. You see, Mr Pascal, once you have considered things closely you realize that nobody actually sins and that therefore nobody is guilty."

Blasius' head reeled, because such ideas had been unknown to him before, although he should have known them. There was indeed nothing wrong with Father Anselme's words, because how could someone be responsible for something he had done without his free will? His own will alone without insight was not free will, but merely the instinct, the main feature of the animal. The living creature in a state without insight was ignorant of the sin. If one's own will was conducted by insight, the sin was impossible.

"Now I think I do understand that one cannot sin without free will. But I still do not understand why somebody can sin because he has free will," Blasius said, because his own brain felt paralyzed and incapable of dealing with the barrage of unexpected ideas.

"People have exactly as much free will as they have insight to use their own will. However, they often rage like dangerous beasts, creating the impression that they have much free will, although very little insight. But this is not so, because the rage of the beast is not the expression of free will, but of the beast's instinctive necessity. The beast is not aware of its own character, therefore it is innocent. Only a creature that is aware of the beast inside itself can have free will. Only then can this creature keep its intrinsic instinctive necessity within bounds, stand above it. When this capability is added to the beast, man is born, because only then that creature – equipped with this insight – stands above its own animal aspect.

He who however, glorifies the beast in himself and thinks that the beast in himself is nobler than the beasts in other individuals and that he should therefore have greater bestial rights than others, does not understand the difference between the beast and man."

"And what is the beast?" Blasius interrupted him, because he felt that Father Anselme meant by 'beast' something that was different from the usual meaning of the word.

"The beast in man is the lack of knowledge of the unity of the world. Whoever lacks the knowledge of the unity of the world cannot understand the idea *that any other person is you yourself wearing different clothing called a body, there-*

fore in a completely different situation. The human body is the unique, specific, concrete situation of man in each individual. To all people who are aware of the unity of the world, the content of this idea is the guide in the strange labyrinth of existence," Father Anselme replied and his face was all peace, radiating a mixture of devoutness and melancholy, as if he had wanted to say: "Life would be more comfortable if insight and wisdom were man's constant companions, but it is good the way it is, because it is the only way it can be."

"Because of the lack of insight, you said, Father, didn't you?" Blasius asked, just to ask something, because in that moment he was not able to ask a reasonable question.

"Yes, Mr Pascal, there lies the entire wretchedness of man, the source of all his misery," replied Father Anselme briefly.

"And what is the situation in this respect like in the Society of Jesus?" asked Blasius.

"We respect the personal feelings each individual cherishes for his God as something fundamentally incomprehensible to all outsiders, and therefore we do not care about what someone feels. We discuss such questions whenever we have the opportunity and thus each of us tries to sharpen his mind by comparing his thoughts with those of others; however, never does any one of us try to win over the others for his own view, because each of us learns first of all that each person has and must have his own inner world. Each one's own inner world has to remain the personal realm of every individual forever, because it can never be understood by outsiders."

Blasius did not say anything.

"The only aspects of an individual that are comprehensible to outsiders are his deeds," added Father Anselme.

Blasius did not make any remarks. But what could he have said, for everything that Father Anselme had said was so simple and so convincing that nothing in his words could be questioned.

"Only because of that and no other reason, we members of the Society of Jesus pay attention only and exclusively to somebody's deeds," continued Father Anselme. "What other people think and believe in is their own business, not ours. In conversation, we try to enrich each other and exchange ideas like gifts, however, we don't care about the destiny of the gifts we have given. What happens in other people's hearts and minds must be respected completely and entirely; the best way of doing that is by not paying any attention to it, because one's innermost feelings can never be understood by anybody. Only those who can profoundly realise that nobody can fully understand another person can respect another human being as well as themselves, as the mystery of all mysteries.

We are a community guided by the idea that human relations should be governed solely by the aforementioned principles."

"Is that your basic insight?" Blasius asked, because the last words of the Father sounded like a final explanation.

A barely perceptible smile crossed Father Anselme's face.

"Something like this," he continued, "can never be the fundamental insight but merely the result of an insight."

"And what is your basic insight?" Blasius asked in a tone that sounded lightly insulting. He was angry with himself that things just explained by Father Anselme had to be explained to him at all. The tone of his question didn't escape Father Anselme; however he answered it as if it had been asked in the most amiable way.

"It's something, Mr Pascal, that the followers of religions as a rule don't know what to do with. It is the insight that God and man create each other and do each other justice. That means that God and man are exactly matched to each other, so that they depend on each other and correspond to each other. In their relation to each other, God and man change to the same extent.

Therefore all the deeds of man that make the dignity and the meaning of human existence grow, do at the same time raise the significance of that which makes human beings so different from all other creatures, although man contains and creates them all and everything else."

"And what would that be?" Blasius asked in the same tone.

"That's the idea of the eternal, which remains unaffected by change, the child and the mother of consciousness."

"But, Father, didn't you want to say ...?" Blasius interrupted, because he wanted to have an immediate explanation for something that affected all religions directly, on which all of them depended.

"You have heard it correctly, Mr Pascal, *which*, not *who* remains unaffected by change. The emergence of this idea is at the same time the birth of man and the birth of God."

"Could you explain that a little more precisely, please?" Blasius asked Father Anselme, because what he had just heard was beguiling.

"That something in which the idea of the eternal arises

becomes man," Father Anselme spoke the strange words slowly, "and the idea of the eternal itself becomes God."

Blasius was silent; his head reeled, because for the first time in his life he heard a neat explanation of how God and man as two poles of the whole are born simultaneously.

"Only this idea and this idea only gives mean to life. Where it is absent, life is lacking meaning, although it may be full of interesting purposes."

Father Anselme paused for a short break here, because he felt that his host needed one. Then he continued, for Blasius did not ask any questions.

"And because all sorts of theologians – both the so-called believers and so-called atheists – cannot have this insight of ours, which cannot be forced by their temporally-religious way of thinking, they hate us."

Blasius was silent. The last words of Father Anselme touched him deeply.

"If one is, however, carried by the feeling born by this idea, by this insight, one simply cannot do anything wrong, because, as already stated, one cannot have an evil intent.

Then one's every deed is holy and noble, because the intent is crucial.

To be guided by this thought, to experience it as a source of the simultaneous birth of man and of God, is the meaning of all endeavours of the members of the Society of Jesus. It is this and no other meaning that justifies all means.

This is what I should like to emphasize to remove those misconceptions that are unfortunately present in so many heads, even of very intelligent people, where there indeed shouldn't be any."

"I suppose you mean *purpose*, Father?" Blasius cut him short to get the matter straight.

"No, Mr Pascal, I mean meaning, *not* purpose."

Blasius stared at Father Anselme, because he could not distinguish between meaning and purpose.

"What is the difference between meaning and purpose, Father?" he said in the manner of a good student again.

"Each purpose is a compulsory constituent element of a dry, dull life, because it ends in itself, a blind alley as it were.

Meaning, on the other hand, is always a gateway to a new world, to a new horizon, leading beyond itself, because it is infinitely more than it usually seems to be.

Purposes are merely separate thought states of the dust, end stations of a fragmented life.

Meaning is a deliberately chosen, suitable spot to take a proper rest and gather strength, in order never to be forced to stop approaching the eternal. It is the moment when you enjoy the fruits of coming closer in that sense – the Korban."

Blasius listened to Father Anselme without stirring an eyelid, without saying anything.

For the first time in his life he felt tossed into a totally unfamiliar landscape and he heard undreamt-of things.

"Is that the case even if someone chooses despicable means to achieve that end?" Blasius asked, for he was well acquainted with the words tirelessly quoted by the enemies of the Society of Jesus to vilify the Jesuits they hated so much and which he himself had used in his latest writings with the same intention.

"Those who interpret these words that way don't understand the essence of the *meaning* I have just spoken about. And because most people do not understand the meaning of these words, we have so many enemies that would readily kill us all, if they had the chance to do that. Recently, an anonymous author published some writings in the form of letters in which he very skilfully and wittily attacks the Society of Jesus," Father Anselme answered calmly.

Blasius gasped but he tried to remain calm and pretended to hear of it for the first time. He was deeply convinced that Father Anselme could not possibly know that he personally was the author of those writings, because he hadn't told anybody about it, not even his closest friends.

He therefore asked Father Anselme to tell him more about it.

"I have read the *Lettres à un provincial* and I must confess that they are very cleverly written, they create confusion as successfully as they sow hatred for certain people whom the author doesn't even know.

The author seems to be someone with a great one-sided talent but lacking the crucial insight that I have just spoken about and therefore inevitably the sense of the whole as well.

For that reason the published letters are pure nonsense coated with a layer of gloss, the product of someone who is completely ignorant of the things he wants to talk about."

He spoke these words quietly and without the slightest trace of anger or bitterness and accompanied them with a barely perceptible hand gesture as if to say that such misunderstandings and people's reactions were not uncommon but – like everything else that happened – rather belonged to human existence.

As he spoke he looked straight into Blasius' eyes, as if he had wanted to say to his interlocutor: Now you know what your writings are worth, Mr Pascal.

Blasius remained silent. He was still trying to pretend that the whole story about *Lettres à un provincial* was something entirely new to him but he failed, because he was not quite sure any more that Father Anselme didn't know who the author was.

"Then in your opinion, Father, there is no God?" he asked, using such a general question in order to direct the conversation away from the *Lettres*.

"The God who there is or who there is not, is the God of religions and their followers. It is the silliest product of ignorance, hence not blasphemy, although it bears all the traits of blasphemy.

Ignorance makes innocent though, because the ignorant are always forgiven; however, it does not protect against punishment; the punishment I mean is a meaningless life."

"But what is the use of your insight in the fight against sin?" Blasius asked, somewhat disparagingly, because Father Anselme's remark about his *Lettres* had hurt him deeply. By asking such a question, he hoped to drive his interlocutor into a corner and show him that even his superior insight was ultimately useless in practical life, because a satisfactory answer seemed impossible to him.

"It is not merely useful, Mr Pascal," said Father Anselme quietly, "it is the only effective remedy against it; however, the path leading to it through the strange jungle of theories and views is not easily perceptible, because it is extremely rarely trodden. The result is that even very intelligent people often have lots of trouble reaching it."

Blasius had not expected such an answer. It sounded good, radiated self-confidence, and above all it was strange and incomprehensible to him. So he asked Father Anselme for a more detailed explanation of what he had just said.

"The sin disappears as soon as one has realized what it is," continued Father Anselme in a calm tone, as if he hadn't been interrupted. He tried again because it was obvious that his interlocutor either hadn't quite understood or retained what had been explained earlier.

"And what remains in its place, Father? A world without sin cannot exist, Father, otherwise..!", interrupted Blasius, and everything he said, resembled more a command than a question, because he felt that Father Anselme's explanations made his own way of thinking untenable, and his world view had started to shake.

"I also heard what you didn't say, Mr Pascal: without sin there is no devil, and without the devil his opponent also disappears.

When expressed in plain language, Mr Pascal, that would mean: God, as spoken of by the religions, is dependent on the existence of the devil and turns out to be unnecessary as soon as the whole religious edifice is subjected to a careful scrutiny."

Blasius was silent.

"Yes, yes, Mr Pascal," continued Father Anselme, "sin is an inevitable concomitant of the personification of God. A master of the world, even if he is ever so gentle and patient, does not cease to be a judge. Therefore, all religious adherents fear eternal damnation and are well-behaved, just because they fear eternal punishment. All the good ones of that sort expect that their supplications, prayers, wringing their hands and their continuous self-abasement and their incessant repetition that they themselves were disgustingly sinful creatures could increase their chances to get a place in paradise."

"And what do the members of the Society of Jesus think about that, Father?" asked Blasius, because he was interested to hear the opinion of those people whom he had criticised and derided, with his enviable brilliance and with his skills sharper than anybody else, without having ever spoken to them before.

The idea that God in all monotheistic religions, including the God in whom he believed, was merely the product of a tremendous misunderstanding, a grave flaw in reasoning, provoked Blasius to learn the views of the Society of Jesus regarding this perhaps crucial question of man. As a mathematician, he valued rigorous mathematical logic above all and was always trying to eliminate the smallest discrepancy even in the most banal situation, because everything that was opposed to mathematical logic bothered him. Perhaps that was the reason why he could not imagine that an intelligent, educated person could have an idea of God that was fundamentally different from his own. Therefore he was deeply convinced that there must have been serious flaws in the reasoning of the Society of Jesus when it came to their idea of God; he himself felt called upon to eliminate such errors. Father Anselme was the best source of information he could imagine when it came to the views of the Jesuits.

"I don't know what the members of the Society of Jesus think about that, however that is of no significance. I only know what they say and, first of all, how they behave in everyday life," answered Father Anselme, and continued.

"The members of the society of Jesus are convinced that blunders do not result from some original sin committed by our ancestors at the very beginning of the human existence but from the conditionality of appearance."

"What do you mean by that?" Blasius asked, because he did not understand the words 'conditionality of appearance'.

"Every appearance is always conditioned by that which we call place and time. We experience that conditionality as a particular way of being," Father Anselme answered.

"I see, but what does that have to do with sin?" Blasius asked another question, for he could not connect space and time with sin and that obviously annoyed him.

"Everything has to do with it and everything is immediately dependent on it, however people are usually not aware of that."

"Could you please explain that more precisely?" Blasius asked in a faltering voice and his hands trembled.

"I am just doing it, Mr Pascal, try to be a little patient, please; each explanation is also conditioned by the frame of place and time and it therefore requires some time," Father Anselme said with a friendly smile, for he had noticed that his host was nervous and impatient.

Blasius did not say anything. He felt embarrassed by his own unnecessary urging and interrupting of his guest.

*

"A particular constellation of forces," Father Anselme continued in the same tone, "can make something appear unsuitable to us, therefore quite often undesirable, even evil. Something else on the other hand appears suitable to us, therefore quite often desirable, even laudable.

Thus all unpleasant experiences of people merge into an idea of a fundamental opponent who does not tolerate unity but rejects and disperses everything, causes chaos and whose main objective is to bring disaster on man.

All welcome and pleasant experiences on the other hand crystallize into an idea of a benevolent being whose main objective is the salvation of man.

These two phantoms created by man become independent and attain paramount importance in the existence of their own creators, determining the meaning of their lives."

"But how have these phantoms you have been speaking about been able to survive and be so effective throughout the human history if they, in fact, do not exist at all?" Blasius asked, because he knew well what an important role God and the Devil had in the world in which he lived.

"The two needn't be anxious about their existence, because the world never lacks unpleasant things and terrible events, which ensure that the presence of the Devil is steadily renewed and strengthened. The short intervals between the unpleasant events are regularly experienced as happy hours, especially if those that preceded them were extremely unpleasant and difficult. Since the time they became aware of themselves, people have been acquainted with the rhythm in which the pleasant alternates with the unpleasant. Even in the most adverse situations, that knowledge makes people confident that after the unpleasant the pleasant will follow. That long experience grants confidence that any time of tribulation – regardless how terrible and how long – must sometime cease, if not during one's lifetime, then definitely after death. It is the mother of hope that some day things will change for the better, either during their lifetime or in the hereafter at the latest. And because people in general do not realize that virtually everything is but a result of a ceaseless, imperceptible interplay of forces, they look for the source of sin somewhere else. There are three possible places where that source can be found. The most obvious source is one's own body with all its desires, emotions and natural troubles that every human being is intimately acquainted with. That is the concrete, tangible source of sin. The abstract source of sin is the Devil as the personification of the fundamental adversary of the good. The third source fills the gap between the concrete and the abstract ones. Our name for that source between is 'the world'. Once we have understood that, we also immediately realise that man is encumbered with a terrible load caused by his own spiritual indolence and a lack of imagination. His own body is then a torture chamber, a dungeon full of sins from which he cannot escape as long as he is alive. Only death can rescue him from it. The world is the palace containing all individual dungeons. The atmosphere pervading the world-palace and man's own torture chamber is the evil spirit. In order to subsist, the human body desires and requires something all the time. To get its wishes fulfilled, it is forced to dance to the music of the world. That means: it is forced to act as the evil spirit wants it. Religion says that man is fundamentally sinful." Father Anselme said and looked at his host with a friendly smile and made a gentle gesture with both hands as if to say: that seems to be the state of affairs.

Blasius was silent. He had nothing to say, because all the explanations offered by Father Anselme were so convincing and, above all, so simple that there was no room for error.

"So everything depends on the interplay of forces, on the constellation of forces," continued Father Anselme.

"Every new constellation of forces we people experience as a new state of the world, each of us in his own way, depending on his personal condition."

Blasius stared at his guest. What Father Anselme was speaking about sounded vaguely familiar to him.

"A certain constellation of forces, Mr Pascal, can be experienced – depending on one's personal situation – as reprehensible or as laudable. Thus, because even the smallest and the most insignificant variation of the interplay of forces means a new constellation, the world is always and everywhere something different; it is always and everywhere experienced in a different way although it is always one and the same world.

One needn't make any effort to perceive the differences; they offer themselves, always and everywhere, because even with the slightest movement of anything the world slips into a different constellation and is experienced by the human mind as change and as differences. And because differences follow each other seamlessly, for our mind everything flows and passes, although it just leaves our personal sphere of perception.

However, to attain the insight that all differences make up the same One, you have to struggle constantly, because that same One is always wrapped in the veil of perpetual change. That's the way back out of the world towards our inside, the return," said Father Anselme.

"I can understand that if one is talking about ordinary things, but can the same principle apply to the absolute, to God?" Blasius asked further, because everything didn't seem entirely clear to him.

"Then all the more, Mr Pascal," said Father Anselme

quietly, "because only in the absolute sense does the full meaning of the principle becomes apparent; in practical life, however, the validity of the principle is felt only partially, sometimes not at all, which is not surprising, because we experience only an infinitesimal part of the whole, a splinter; splinters are always sharp-edged and pointed, can easily sting and hurt, cause pain. Therefore, life hurts, sometimes as power, sometimes as impotence, sometimes as abundance, sometimes as poverty."

For a few moments both were silent.

*

"You said, Father, that sin was a direct consequence of the religious understanding of God, didn't you?" Blasius asked further, because he needed some additional explanations. "Could you please also explain that a little more precisely, because I didn't quite understand it? And what is the conception of God in the Society of Jesus? Has the God of the Society of Jesus anything to do with sin?"

Blasius showered Father Anselme again with the previously asked questions. Some sounded like a desperate plea for an explanation while others were rather arrogant, even insulting.

"With each growth of human insight," continued Father Anselme in the same gentle tone, "the glory of God, as understood by the Society of Jesus, also increases. The members of the Society consider themselves children of Abraham by trying to be aware of the essence of the human being. That is, they try to live after the shining example of Abraham with the idea that man creates his world and his God by being himself created by his God and his world."

"But that is not religious, Father, and you belong to a religion."

Blasius' words sounded like a reproach, as if he had wanted to say that the attitude of the Society of Jesus was hypocritical, godless.

"That is not quite how it is, Mr Pascal," said Father Anselme in a calm voice as usual, "we are considered to be members of a religion but that is not the same thing; the misunderstanding is not our fault.

If several members of the Society of Jesus happen to be in the temporal and spatial sense close to each other, they behave like a group, the members of which help each other, thus easily creating the impression of being almost an insular sect.

Only very few know that the members of the Society of Jesus might as well be alone and they often are; however, each of our members knows that somewhere in the world there are other members whose hearts beat in the same rhythm, although they never meet one another. This knowledge, Mr Pascal, this awareness is the invisible bond that we all are bound to one another. That doesn't require any cards or badges. Our only distinctive marks are our deeds. As far as the idea of God is concerned, each one of us creates it as best as he can, each of us is addressed by God as it suits him best."

Blasius did not like Father Anselme's explanation, because he felt excluded, although he did not like the Society of Jesus and should, in fact, have been glad that he could not be a member of the peculiar club, which apparently wasn't one.

*

"Is it not hypocrisy," Blasius launched a new attack, "when the confessors of the Society of Jesus impose prayers on the penitents intended to serve as repentance? Why prayers, why repentance, if, according to your explanation, Father, sin as such doesn't exist, but is only experiences of certain constellations of forces?"

Blasius' tone was not friendly. His face was pale and his dark eyes looked even darker than usual.

"You see, Mr Pascal," continued Father Anselme in the same calm and friendly tone, "we in the Society of Jesus are well aware that most people do not know what to make of the God I have already spoken quite a lot about. Most of them are still just herd animals, they need a herd leader, a boss, a Lord, a King, even a king of kings; in their heaven they need a heavenly Lord and here on earth, a guardian. Most people lack that insight I spoke about at the beginning, and that scarcity is the origin of the whole human misery; that has already been said, too."

Blasius said nothing, but what could he have said? He was well aware that his education, his knowledge and his intellectual capabilities were considerably greater than those of other people, and yet he himself had to ask countless additional questions and needed numerous additional explanations to understand just a part of that which Father Anselme had tried to explain to him.

"These are bitter adversaries of the Society of Jesus," continued Father Anselme. "On the one hand, they say that for God everything is determined in advance because everything was being done by his will, at his behest, and therefore God knows everything that will ever happen, everything, down to the smallest and most insignificant little thing, perceptible and imperceptible. On the other hand, they are not tired of trying to mollify their God and induce him to act in a way that is favourable to them with all sorts of incantations and ritual magic, which they describe as prayer and worship."

Blasius was silent. His face seemed to have turned yellow and paler than usual. What he heard from the mouth of the lean, ascetic-looking Father was against his religious conviction; however, his strictly mathematically working brain regarded it as consistent and incontestable.

Father Anselme noticed that his host was indeed sad, but that he had no objection. The teacher in his veins forced him to continue with his explanation, for he felt that the moment was extremely convenient for a particular purpose: his interlocutor, to whom he was explaining views generally unknown, was someone whose brilliant mind and peculiar assertions had a very good chance of waking interest in numerous people looking for answers sometime in the future, and he therefore should be well informed.

He felt that his pale, gravely ill host was a suitable tube through which the juice of his explanations could flow. That juice, the strange substance, promised to cause numerous fruits to ripen and to satiate all those who would be looking for satisfactory answers to the most important questions in human life sometime in the future.

"Doesn't that show clearly, Mr Pascal, how little the adversaries of the Society of Jesus trust the love of their God? Do they not consider their God a despot who has to be ceaselessly besought, who however, is in no way obliged to hear even the most ardent imploring of his miserable creatures? When, in spite of all the beseeching and prayers, sacrifices and supplications, their God allows that they meet with the greatest thinkable tragedy, they justify the decision of their God and declare themselves, his creatures, guilty although he has created them in his ultimate wisdom and his ultimate goodness, just as he wanted to create them in his omnipotence.

That the same God to whom they pray allows offenders and criminals to carry out their terrible work cannot startle them awake, or free them from the phantom whose slaves they are, because they are lacking insight. Yes, Mr Pascal, the human tragedy resulting from that lacking is complete.

Although their omniscient God must have known exactly how some day they would behave as living organisms, they blame themselves for everything and try to defend the goodness and infallibility of their God. At the same time they hate those who have done them injustice with the permission of their all-merciful and almighty God."

Blasius did not stir and remained silent. What could he say? Father Anselme said nothing that might have contradicted his own conception of God. His God was also omnipotent, omniscient, most benevolent, most gracious and most merciful. That was known to him. And yet his God permitted the cruellest and the most disgusting as often as he did the most beautiful and the most agreeable. He demanded complete submission and subjugation from his subjects; however, he owed them nothing.

And even the slightest dissatisfaction of his subjects with what they have been bestowed upon by God was nothing less than a mortal sin, loss of the right to be allowed to hope for eternal salvation.

"That is how the adversaries of the Society of Jesus think and feel, believe and live," continued Father Anselme.

"If they, instead, tried to attain a higher insight, they would probably stop being our adversaries, would perhaps join us in our views. That is our conviction. Then each step, each breath and each act of every one of them would be a prayer, a conversation with the highest that one regards as such at one's personal level of insight; that highest is exactly what creates the essence of the human being and what itself is created by that same human being. The life of each and every one of them would be deeper and nobler, not torn to pieces by purposes but filled with meaning, just for the greater glory of the highest, which one seeks to approach.

This relentless seeking to get closer to the highest would be the sacrifice. That is exactly the meaning of the word 'Korban' or 'sacrifice' in the language of the world in which the Christian teaching was born.

However, in the world we know, the word 'sacrifice' is understood in all monotheistic religions as something that causes division and hatred, because each religion has its own way of making sacrifices and performing rites, which are very efficient when it comes to separating people and smothering love.

When we assign prayers that should be meditated on after confession, which should bring about a conversion, we are well aware how small the chance is that such conversion will indeed occur. However, we also know that such conversion is never ruled out. If it happens just once anywhere at any time, the countless attempts haven't been in vain. The so-called prayers have, of course, nothing to do with the imploring and begging designed to reach the ears of some supernatural ruler of the world and king of kings and make him propitious and generous. The fact that our adversaries consider, for example, the Lord's Prayer a carefully drafted begging formula is not our fault. Instead of prayer, one should rather speak of contemplation that could help the people to wonder at the world and life. In the original language of the world, from which the Scripture is sprung – therefore the whole Christian teaching as well – to pray means to wonder. In each person that marvels at life and the world the conversion has taken place. By conversion we in the Society of Jesus mean turning away from the life-hostile, destructive, temporally-religious way of thinking and gaining the insight that God and man create each other, that they come into being through each other and that this mutual act of creation is identical with the creation of the world. Seen that way, every increase in human insight at the same time enhances the glory of the eternal and functions as its revival and subsistence. I hope I have answered your question."

Blasius' feeling of being excluded was so strong that he experienced the Father's explanation as an insult.

"But where do you in the Society of Jesus go once you are dead if you do not believe in the Lord in heaven who for some has prepared eternal joy in paradise, for others eternal torment in hell? I understand from your words that there is, in fact, no sin, but that there are only cases where people take false steps which result from a lack of insight," he asked Father Anselme.

The latter hesitated a moment, and a charming ironical smile crossed his narrow face – the question was somewhat clumsy, not to be expected from someone whose writings were highly appreciated in the salons of Paris, not least because of their elegant language. Father Anselme had waited for that question, because it obtruded itself as a logical consequence of the previous conversation; Blasius simply was bound to ask it.

"We go where we are supposed to, but we do not rack our brains over it. We do what we can and what we cannot is neither our duty, nor our concern," said Father Anselme.

Again, there was a short pause, filled with utter silence. Another door was closed before Blasius, and access seemed even more impossible than before. Without thinking twice, he tried again to find an entrance gate.

"But if there is a paradise and a hell in a religious sense, which you, Father, apparently do not take seriously, then the members of the Society of Jesus are not particularly clever, because you do not serve the God who has not merely created heaven and earth but also paradise and hell, which are waiting for all people after the Day of Judgement."

"We cannot make any comments on the religious ideas of entertainment centres and penal institutions in the hereafter," said Father Anselme quietly with a slightly impish smile. The gentle movements of his pale, slender hands underlined his deep conviction of being right.

"Our adversaries seem to be better versed in such affairs. We know nothing about it, we are still very young as a registered society, although we, as an idea, are as old as man himself; his birth was also ours, for we held his heels firmly while we were being pulled out of the body of our common mother in order to find our way back home together."

Blasius shuddered. He had never heard anything like that before. The words of the strange little man were overwhelming. He was silent.

"Ignatius has even registered something under our name, however, that is without any significance. We existed before we were registered, and we do not stop existing when we are prohibited, which will undoubtedly happen again and again. Nor do we start anew when we are officially allowed to work. What Loyola registered under our name has nothing to do with us; nor has that which is forbidden or allowed respectively."

Blasius was not sure whether he had understood all that Father Anselme was speaking about, however he felt that all his guest had said drew its life from a completely different unity that was based on a completely different way of thinking, entirely foreign to him and probably to all people he knew. He suddenly felt Father Anselme's words, whom he personally had sent for, as an assault on his own world and all the values in it. That's why he tried to defend his threatened world with all the means at his disposal.

"But if there is – in spite of all your considerations and insights – yet an eternal happiness in paradise and eternal torment in hell, then it is worth staking everything on one card and putting all one's eggs in one basket and take refuge in the God religions are telling us about and doing everything possible in order to gain the infinite wealth, isn't it, Father?"

And without waiting for Father Anselme's response he continued.

"What can be won by that is so infinitely precious that – compared with it – all troubles and efforts in this life are without any weight whatsoever. Because of the infinite value of the potential win one simply must play and throw the dice; it doesn't matter how small the probability appears to be to achieve the infinite gain.

Do play, Father! You can't lose anything, but you can win everything! Try, Father, to explain to your Society, what I am telling you now! There probably nobody who thinks about what the game is and hardly anyone is aware of how high the potential profit is! I have deliberated everything carefully, Father, and I have calculated everything precisely!"

Without being aware of it, Blasius had stood up during his fiery speech and had approached his guest so that his face almost touched that of Father Anselme, and his gesticulating right hand almost did not allow the neat, ascetic-looking, very calm, little man to see his host's face.

He suddenly retired in small, slow steps, because he seemed to have said what he had intended to say.

He sat down again on the chair where he had been sitting at the beginning of the conversation.

"I am afraid, Mr Pascal, that hardly anything of that kind should be explained to us in the Society," said Father Anselme, and nothing indicated that the impassioned, forceful speech of his host had had any influence on him, "for we do not throw dice with our God. We and our God always have the same share in the profits, always belong to the same party and therefore always fight with each other, never against each other. Our life serves the glory of God and our God serves us by sanctifying our actions, which strengthens and ennobles our lives; thus thanks to our higher insight our God appears to us even higher. Above all, we don't expect anything, for we are always at the winning post; we don't hope, because we know that God sends us only the possible. And we do not make any contracts with our God, which the adversaries of the Jesuits always do, because they cannot distinguish between God and a businessman. By the way, this is a specialty of religions: religious people do something and expect a kind of reward for their being well-behaved or they don't do certain things, because they fear punishment, in any form."

Blasius was silent.

"In the heaven of our adversaries," continued Father Anselme, "seems to flourish the same seductive lottery and betting which they love so dearly here on earth, as well as their strange, venal judiciary. The divinity of the Jesuits, Mr. Pascal, is eternity itself, the pure opposite of any calculation."

Blasius had played his last and strongest card, but it could not penetrate the shield behind which the small, thin Father lived and prayed, acted and loved in security; his cingulum of certainty was wide and firm.

Blasius looked at his elegant clock, rose at the same time and remarked that it was already quite late. On the one hand, his words sounded like an apology – that is what they were indeed intended for; on the other hand, the undertone in them was a suggestion to end the conversation and the Father's visit as well.

"It's pretty late. Please don't feel offended, Father, but I am in terrible pain, I have a bad headache. I am no longer fit for a conversation, I must have a rest."

*

The small, thin man stood up from his chair simultaneously with Blasius. His movement resembled very much that of a shadow, which follows – according to the usual human experience – simultaneously the movements of the body on which it indeed depends, with which it, however, has nothing to do. One might have got the impression that they had practiced together the act of simultaneous standing up and agreed how and when to perform it a long time before. Blasius, who had noticed it immediately, was petrified and stood rooted to the spot for a moment.

"I can believe you, Mr Pascal, my limbs are also quite tired, I am no longer young," replied Father Anselme, "another time we might have an even better opportunity; in another story, in a play perhaps, where no comment is necessary, because there one must act in accordance with one's own internal necessity and is therefore completely free."

Blasius listened to Father Anselme's strange words and did not reply.

"There," Father Anselme continued, "from where both of us come, there must be many a one of our sort, who can hardly wait to be allowed to have their say and tell something beautiful that can both delight and instruct. We must, of course, be considerate of them and let them also have their say. I am very obliged to you for the edifying conversation. Goodbye, Mr Pascal, and good night. Laudetur!"

"Semper Laudetur! Good night, Father, and thank you so much for your effort."

"Father Anselme proceeded in small steps towards the door. His cassock reached almost to the ground so that his feet were not visible. He seemed weightless as he was moving forward without any effort, just floating, as it were.

"Louise," Blasius said, just loud enough for the servant who was staying in the room next to his to hear him.

"Would you see Father Anselme to the door, please?"

The maid appeared at the door even before Blasius had finished his sentence and disappeared with Father Anselme down the stairs.

Blasius stayed in the corridor, in front of his door until the parting words of the visitor and the servant had ceased. He could hear the front door snap shut and the key turn twice in the lock. Then he went back to his room, closed the door and sank into the chair at his desk.

He was tired, exhausted in the truest sense of the word, because he was empty. The conversation with Father Anselme was not an ordinary one. He had never experienced anything like that before. Everything he had regarded before the conversation as proven, reliable and irrefutable now appeared to him stupid, fundamentally wrong, worthless, miserable. He was ashamed. Some particularly sharp-witted people were living in his vicinity and he had had a unique opportunity to sharpen his mind in conversation with them; that was exactly what he had always wished; he had let that unique opportunity slip.

Only now, after so many silly and unpleasant things had happened, he had made their acquaintance through a member of the Society of Jesus. It was simply too late, because he couldn't make amends for all he had done before the visit of Father Anselme.

Instead of seeking to make their acquaintance and discuss with them the most delicate questions that man has been asking since he became aware of his human nature; instead of enjoying that particular privilege that every alert mind always dreams of, he spent his precious time with the people of Port-Royal, who claimed something that was of no use whatsoever for those who were looking for an answer.

"Why could I not realise straightaway that man loses the finest part of his nature when he becomes governed by the feeling that for him everything is determined in advance and that he is completely dependent on the grace of God, which the Jansenists claim?" he thought.

"Could I not think for myself? Was it necessary that a Jesuit Father explains to me that the doctrine of predestination and grace is an expression of complete humiliation of infantile people? If everything down to the smallest detail in the life of man is fixed before the creation of the world, for all eternity, his salvation and his fall, then what of man is left? For what can he still be responsible at all? Was I so stupid that I could not immediately notice how preposterous such an attitude is? I have embittered the end of my father's life; I have made him spend the last moments of his life in hell; I have robbed his life of its meaning and I have driven him to despair, to the most absurd death. Yes, I have killed my own begetter by destroying his zest for life. Do I still have a right to exist? Arnauld would now probably say that my deed had also been fixed before the time began. Maybe that's right, but if that is so, then I'm useless as a person, I have nothing to say, I am nothing, I am less than that!"

***

Whether he had had a long sleep or just a short slumber, he did not know, but he suddenly sat up, moved his chair closer to the desk, grabbed the pen and started to write. He did it quite hastily, as if afraid he would forget what he wanted to write down. His brain worked feverishly; his hands could hardly follow.

He put the pen down again, leaned back comfortably and just spoke his thoughts in a strange soliloquy half aloud, half to himself.

"All the educated and conceited of Paris have read the *Lettres* and they all find them amusing, witty and brilliant. All admire my language, my acumen. The only ones who derive benefit from it are the people of Port-Royal."

Shaking his head regretfully, he continued with his monologue.

"I was a fool, because I took for gospel truth what Arnauld told me about the Jesuits instead of speaking to some of them first and thus getting first-hand information about their views."

He leaned even further back, gazing at the ceiling. It was only faintly illuminated by the dim candlelight. The corners of the room were almost completely dark. Nothing stirred in the room; the upright flame of candle proved it. The only thing he could hear besides the ticking of the watch in the pocket of his coat was the beating of his own heart.

"What should I do now? Is there at all anything that could be done?" he asked himself aloud.

"The whole thing reminds me of the debate between Descartes and me: everybody thinks I'm the winner, and only I know about my own misery.

Shall I write new, corrected, apologizing *Lettres* and ask the Society for forgiveness?

No, no, no, I cannot possibly do that. What is done is done.

Now we are in the final act.

My drama draws to an end; other worlds are emerging already.

Time's running short.

Asking for forgiveness would be total self-denial, self-abasement, which I could not possibly bear.

I've done quite badly and made a pitiable figure in my conversation with Father Anselme.

It was me who sent for him with the intention to pump him and to make fun of him.

Father Anselme is right: the lack of insight is the source of all evil.

It is a good thing that nobody listened to us, otherwise all my misery would become known to everybody."

No sooner had he uttered the last word than he tapped his forehead with the palm of his hand.

"Oh, how stupid I am! There is always someone listening, even if you do not see them. Then even more than normal, otherwise nobody would write one single reasonable line about me.

If all members of the Society of Jesus are like Father Anselme, then they are too high for us, unattainable, for their insights seem to be of a higher nature. Only now I understand why the Jesuits are so much hated: they are too rich for the poverty that surrounds them, and their wealth is of the rarest kind; it cannot be easily distributed among the poor; therefore there is no balance, and that seems to be the source of all suffering."

*

Suddenly the door opened, very quietly indeed, but he could still hear it, because the house was totally silent.

Gilberte came in without knocking. Her face and clothes showed that she was still up.

"Sorry, brother, to disturb you, but two men from Port-Royal are waiting outside – they would like to see you."

"Tell them I cannot receive anybody," he said without looking at her.

The way Blasius responded to her announcement surprised her very much, because up to that very moment he used to abandon even the most important work if someone from Port-Royal wanted to speak to him.

Now he did not even ask who the visitors were and what they wanted but simply refused to speak to them.

"What could have induced Blasius to such a reaction?" Gilberte thought as she ran down the stairs to tell the unwanted visitors that he couldn't receive them.

*

"I am now in the last act of my life story," Blasius continued, speaking to himself.

"Every second is precious."

What he felt when he uttered those words is, of course, not known, nor is our intention to try to find out. Instead, we will open the gate and let in what he said. If we do that impartially and without reservation, it may happen that the hidden content of his utterance brings about in us that which gave life to what he said, that the created creates its creator.

"If now I do not succeed in understanding what I am, if I am anything at all; what the meaning of my life is, if there is any at all and where I shall go, if I ever go anywhere at all, then it will never happen, because the fourth decade in human life is reserved for attaining insight. What follows after that is the time in which one should enjoy what he has attained."

He looked at the clock. It was already past midnight.

"What Father Anselme told me yesterday is too much for my coach, it requires a completely different road, otherwise the axle might break because of the weight of the load. The road on which I am moving is too bumpy, it has too many potholes."

Blasius rubbed his temples. He felt a sort of shock of a wave, the strength of which his boat could not resist.

The craziest ideas concerning probability, which he had been dealing with for years, now received a new impetus from the strange conversation with a Jesuit Father and appeared to him infinitely more important and pregnant with meaning than he could ever have imagined.

Above all, something appeared on the horizon, which, on the one hand – warning of danger – discouraged him from pursuing that idea, on the other hand – for reasons of clarity – urged him to continue dealing with it. He had a feeling of only now being aware of what was contained in the idea of probability. Once there was the slightest probability – no matter how small, Father Anselme said – that someone was not solely responsible for his actions, he was innocent.

"Never before have such thoughts crossed my mind," he thought, "but it is just this thought of Father Anselme's which smells quite strongly of predetermination, which is in principle rejected by the Society of Jesus.

However, he took the matter further in a different way.

Man could, indeed, choose, he said, however, his choice was linked to the choice of all others taken together. Thus all chose for each individual, and the choices of all others were influenced by the choice of each individual. Therefore, all people formed a single fate community of freely-choosing people who were inevitably interdependent, regardless of whether they were aware of that, whether they thought one way or another.

Yes, yes, yes, it is the interplay of forces, of all forces, the constellation of forces, always a particular and always a different one. This marvellous interplay of forces brings everything about, also our thoughts and our feeling that our world is just as it appears to us, that once it looked different, that it could be different from what it appears to be and that some day it will be different."

Blasius remained silent for a while turning the idea over in his mind again and trying to check it carefully.

"It is free choice," he continued with his meditation, "due to which – according to Father Anselme's opinion – each individual is bound and therefore responsible. Because – ultimately – all others participate in the choice of each individual, all people are responsible for everything, never a single person."

He sighed. He almost became angry with himself, because he had failed to realize all that before; however the anger dissolved in the insight he had just attained, that he himself – like all other individuals – was a child of the entire humanity, in which he was nestled and through which alone he could be what he was; for all his thoughts were born in that same humanity, also the thought that the things were just as they appeared to him, just as he thought they were.

The weight of these thoughts forced him to take a short break again and take a breath.

"Without other people no single person would be possible; there wouldn't be any responsibility, because there wouldn't be anybody to help or harm," he continued with his meditations.

"Not even this last thought of mine could occur. Only vessels of pure emptiness, filled with ignorant innocence, present only in human consciousness as living creatures and things, which neither are a world nor know any, would be the content of that which remained, if man disappeared.

Yes, yes, yes, only now I understand it: the idea that something is or is not, is a purely human affair.

Even the thought that there might be something without man is merely a human idea, which appears and disappears together with man.

And what could be said against this assertion? Not very much, in fact. At most, that even this assertion is merely a human construction, which therefore shouldn't be taken seriously.

However, if I consider this objection carefully, I come to the conclusion that this most subtle argument itself is the best and safest proof of the correctness of what it calls into question.

Father Anselme visited me at my request, because I wanted to confess. Did I confess? Do I feel any form of relief or remorse? I do not know. But I know one thing: now I'm in another world. Is it my fortune or misfortune that I got into Father Anselme's net of thoughts? I cannot judge that either. I'm sure, however, that I am surrounded by the net of his thoughts, because now I see everything in a different light.

If it is the case, as Father Anselme said, that even the smallest probability of innocence suffices to render an individual fundamentally innocent, then there are neither reliable standards nor a binding morality for everybody, because they always depend on the level of insight of each individual. For me, this is a completely new world view, an entirely new way of thinking.

Then it must be considered to be true that even the smallest probability can simultaneously trigger and prevent, and thus participate in the creation of, that which we experience as our reality, as our world.

In that case even without the smallest and apparently the least important element, the world cannot be as it is.

But if the world as it is must unconditionally contain, and if it as unconditionally must not lack even the seemingly smallest and the least important element, then nothing is, in fact, unimportant or trivial. Then it is only our way of experiencing something as such in our own particular concrete situation. And just as we experience it, so it is, because it is only man who believes he knows that something is a particular way, that it could be this or that or some other way.

Only man thinks that he does or that he does not know something, that other creatures can or that they cannot know, that they do or do not exist, that in the past they did or did not exist, as well as that sometime in the future they will or will not exist.

With each change of our experiencing the world, of our

world view, the world changes as well. I have never doubted that the world constantly changes; however, I have never been aware of the fact that the content, the meaning of the word 'change' is present only in the human mind.

In this sense, the entire world is no less the product of man than man is the work of the entire world.

We are the creators of where, of when, of how, of why and wherefore; all that blends and amalgamates only in and through man's mind alone to something, more precisely: to what we call our world."

*

For the second time Blasius was shaken out of his thoughts, for Gilberte had entered again. This time she also did it without knocking first. She had done it with good conscience, for the importance and urgency of what she wanted to tell him seemed great enough to justify it.

"I beg your pardon, brother," she said, obviously very excited, "the two gentlemen of Port-Royal are still waiting outside; they say it is about something extremely important."

Blasius raised his head and said with a gravely earnest expression that he would not receive anybody. Then he lowered his head again and continued his monologue.

Gilberte said nothing and silently left the room.

*

"How silly I was to consider my experiments concerning air pressure and the void very important, even epoch-making.

And I was even sillier to believe that only that which Arnauld was telling me was deep and right. I think it is only now dawning on me what the real state of affairs is."

The thoughts he had just had in his mind and the feeling they created mingled in his innermost being with all the other hidden thoughts and feelings that he had ever had and ever experienced and by which he had ever been inspired and carried. Unintentionally and without any conceivable reason, he touched his breast with his left hand and suddenly paused as if petrified: the sheet of paper he had sewn into the lining of his coat crackled so loudly that he could hear it clearly. He was not a little surprised at it, because immediately after he had sewn it in, it seemed to be so soft and mellow that he did not hear it when tightening and buttoning the coat. And now, suddenly, it was so loud, much louder than the crackling of a new leaf when crumpled in the hand. He could not understand it and shook his head, because something that had been born in a vision and chosen to be an eternal, immutable companion now made itself heard as if trying to get out; thus everything resembled a little labour pain announcing the arrival of a new world.

"The first thing said about God in the Scripture is that he created the world," he thought.

"All other characteristics attributed to God that are found in the Scriptures like love, goodness, mildness, severity, righteousness and many others appear only later in the text, as addenda so to speak," he pondered. He could not understand what made him have such ideas, but now he knew that they were connected with and sprung from all his other ideas so that it would not have been appropriate to try to find their origin, for they did not have any particular one.

Was it because of the might of the insight which he had just struggled through, or for some other reason that could not be made out, that suddenly he began to tremble all over? His hasty gestures betrayed that he was trying to do something immediately, something that seemed extremely important to him and therefore tolerated no delay.

He took a clean sheet of paper and wanted either to continue writing or to start a completely new text, when the door opened, faster and more energetically than ever before.

Gilberte was standing in the door. Her attitude revealed that this time she was determined not to leave empty-handed.

"Brother," she said, cried, in fact, "you must come! They are still waiting! It is not just about something important, it is about something much more than that, they told me!"

The effect that her words had on her brother, who was pale and emaciated by illness, surprised her so much that she was frightened.

"Shut the door, please! Come again only when I call you!" he said with an earnest expression, which prevented her from making any gesture or adding a single word to her request.

Shocked and appalled, she shut the door softly and walked away with small steps.

In the corridor, she stopped. Only a few moments before, she was firmly resolved to make her brother come round and give in; now, however, she was so overwhelmed by his expression and the manner in which he had sent her away that she did not know what to do. She knew that her brother had always put everything he had, including himself, at the disposal of the Jansenists; therefore it was even less comprehensible to her that, all of a sudden, he was not even willing to speak to the men from Port-Royal, although they apparently had a very special concern and obviously needed his help.

Her brother had always been ill and had suffered from terrible headaches almost constantly. His pale, pain-stricken face was familiar to her; however, this time he was in a state he had never been in before. His face was that of a dying madman who in some moment of solemn initiation had attained an insight that assigned him a task, which in his eyes was more important than anything else in the world and which could be done only by him and by him only, for after a brief time of silence and enlightenment the never-ending darkness would follow, the sheer impossibility of changing anything.

"My God! My poor brother! He looks terrible. He has never spoken to me like that. I wish I knew what is going on in his mind," she spoke quietly to herself.

Then she slowly descended the stairs and disappeared into the darkness of the basement.

*

"No, I have not forgotten it! Now I believe I have realized what one should realize during one's life-time: man is, in fact, the creator of the world, the actual scene of the entire world happening, the knot in which usual logic cannot find its way. He is the creator of conception of time and its layers, hence of the idea that something has already happened and that something will happen, and of the layer between, in which actual happenings are just taking place. He knows about the power of the word, the image and the sound. He knows about the fantasy, of its glory and of the dangers lurking in it. He is also the creator of the hidden, which he himself springs from and to which he owes his human existence. Therefore he is the spitting image of the divinity, neither more nor less than the spitting image, therefore identical to it.

Yes, yes, yes, identical with it, one and the same! That is the key to all the key questions! That this one-and-the-same is usually thought of as separated results from the inevitable distance as a prerequisite of experiencing. It is the distance between the experiencing subject and the experienced object. The creation of this gap is identical with the birth of man, for only human beings are aware of themselves as well as of that which is the opposite of their own self and which they call world. This distance, this gap can be overcome only by human beings, not abolished mind you, but overcome. This overcoming is the human assignment. This can only happen if the principal is at the same time the agent who carries out the commission.

Now the only question that remains to be clarified is how man as the creator of the world come into being, or better, what the origin of the key is.

Those who succeed in clarifying this question, that is, who allow the birth of man in their own mind, become conscious creators of the world. All others who cannot allow that birth do also create a world, however without being aware of that; they must starve, because they are not aware of the enormous quantities of the finest food they have in stock."

He leaned far back in his chair so that his neck rested on the upper rounded surface of the backrest, his gaze toward the ceiling, closed his eyes and laid both palms on his face. The iridescence of the world disappeared.

"Existence is something absolutely beguiling: he who does not realize what he himself is revels in the fleeting multitude, enjoys the happiness of the beast in the fold, has no idea of the eternal and remains – despite all the religious, philosophical, scientific and other systems – in the pen of the animal paradise.

Who, on the other hand, realizes what he is, loses the animal paradise and gains the other, the human, which assumes the name eternity, as soon as it is gained. This loss of animal paradise is identical with the birth of man.

Everything that belongs to human existence and to the human world view springs from the wonderful interplay of forces. In that interplay there is something that can both completely confuse and completely explain. It is the insight that even the smallest probability is sufficient, for both ways are sufficient: it can cause everything, and it can also prevent everything; therefore it is doubly valid. Seen that way, the smallest probability is a couple or rather *the* couple.

Now I understand!" he cried for joy, because he had won the insight behind the fleeting world show. There he believed he had found the source of everything, even of the idea that things were just what he now considered them to be. That source of all and everything and the scene of the entire world happening was he himself.

"Now I understand why everything must always be undecided, always uncertain until it happens. And it has happened only when it becomes part of the human world view, kept in the time-drawer called the past.

Only then, yes, only then!" he cried again, because the insight he had just got seemed to have completely overwhelmed him.

"Only then, that is *after* the event, it becomes clear that nothing has ever been undecided, never uncertain and that happening and not happening have never been in balance. In other words, the pans of the world scales have never been in balance. The pan that has always overweighed has been the one in favour of the course of the world – otherwise the world would not exist, for man would not exist to name the things and to attribute them their properties.

The other pan, the one of not happening – merely an object of thought – is always empty, therefore, irrelevant, because what does not happen cannot become part of the human life experience either. It only serves to create world models as the theoretical opposite of what happens. That is the hypothetical antimatter; it would be if it were, it would exist if it were there. It is the content of human speculation, the void not tolerated by nature, because the latter is the creating happening itself.

The most delicate difference, the slightest preponderance in favour of the happening is the affirmative, the crucial aspect of the world, because it decides that everything is just as it is, and it is for everyone just as it seems to them to be.

And all that occurs only after it has happened, yes, after it has happened, because even light as the fastest messenger also needs some time to report. The reports of the light and of other messengers are for us the events, the content of the world!"

He raised both hands high above his head and slapped his palms against each other.

"Likewise, I understand only now what is meant by that glorious place in the Holy Scripture, where it is said that man can see only the back of the divinity, never its face: the back is the past, which we – only after the event – experience as the present and which we then, as our personal experience, put in our personal history drawer.

The finest distinction between the contents of the pans of the world scale, which is beyond all measuring and which therefore cannot be affected by presumption, is always greater than nothing and smaller than any imaginable magnitude that can be expressed by any numbers.

Father Anselme has said that the infinitesimal affirmative probability is the core of the world mystery, of the entire cosmic happening. It is the immeasurable source from which the whole world springs continuously, a continuous explosion as it were, in which the beginning and the end are always united. Those who do not understand this try desperately to calculate and find out when the world started and when it will end. That is probably the most abysmal state of ignorance in which the human mind can be.

The idea of the omnipotence of the infinitely small probability is crazy! It paralyzes and provokes at the same time.

If that is so, then it would be possible, though hardly conceivable, to take blindfolded a single marked grain of sand with a suitable pair of tweezers designed to take just one single grain at a time out of an enormous container – for example, as big as our earth – that is full of sand – at the first attempt.

That is very improbable, however, not impossible.

And the probability of successfully repeating the same procedure – after a vigorous mixing of the sand each time – as many times as is the number of sand grains in the container?

The probability is there, of course, unimaginably smaller, but even there the possibility is not ruled out completely, even there it is infinitely greater than zero."

What such considerations provoked in his ailing, aching, feverish brain, which was extremely good at figures, is impossible to imagine, and to assert anything in that respect would be just meaningless speculation.

Again he lifted both arms as high as he could, so that they stuck up like two candles, looked up and pressed both hands, outstretched and fingers spread, against each other; he remained in that position for a while.

Then he let his hands fall onto his skinny thighs.

"I have never felt mathematical considerations so appealing," he thought, "and all that was triggered in me by Father Anselme. Is it conceivable, for example," he continued with his thoughts, inventing and deliberating ever new and ever crazier degrees of improbability, "that such a magnificent building like the Notre-Dame Cathedral of Paris comes into being by chance, totally unintended and unplanned, with all its hewn stone blocks, flying buttresses, demons, portal figures, ornaments and all sorts of stained rose windows ..? That substances randomly and without any intention unite and make structures, which then – again haphazardly – merge to even more complex, separate elements by motions, frictions, and connections of some kind? That all that gets united by pure chance in an amazing edifice..?"

He had already stopped writing down what he was thinking about and muttering to himself, because all he was considering was so stunning and enrapturing that it did not tolerate the tangible world and therefore no understanding either.

"The chance that something like that happens without any plan or intention is unimaginably small, however, it is greater than zero – it suffices," he continued.

"The more I think about it the more I grow dizzy and the more I realize what the members of the Society of Jesus are guided by in their life. They seem to be aware of all such abysmal depths. They obviously attained a long time ago what I have always been dreaming of.

If intelligent educated people among those supporters of the Reformation, who are serious about it, knew how wonderful, how stunning the views of the Jesuits are, how completely different, how incomparably higher and deeper than all the stuff the so-called Christian world is acquainted with, they would immediately abandon their theological drivel based on ignorance and strive with all their fervour to get to know what I had the privilege to learn from Father Anselme, thanks to the fortunate circumstance that I am hopelessly ill and therefore perhaps secretly wanted to confess.

And what is the case with so-called living substance, the living creatures in this respect? How infinitely improbable it seems to me that – by the pure free play of chance – the materials get mixed together in such a way that a violet or a rose, a bird or a sheep originates from it!

The idea numbs my mind, and my imagination, normally so reliable, which has never forsaken me in juggling with numbers, is simply absent, has obviously no business to be here.

Without exaggeration, I find the vanishingly small probability that such a marvel of architecture like the Cathedral Notre-Dame of Paris comes into being by mere chance as absolute certainty when compared with the probability that an organism arises by chance.

But even that staggeringly small chance again seems to be the purest certainty, when compared with the probability that substances combine and unite in such a way that abstract thinking springs from their connection and combination, that which we call consciousness without being aware of what we, in fact, say.

And if I think out and consider all that carefully, I realize that this very consciousness, our conscious being, gives birth to everything else, yes, to everything, without any exception, even to the thought itself that this consideration is true."

*

Blasius paused here. His look, apparently directed straight ahead, was fixed on nothing; he saw nothing, though his eyes were wide open. He heard nothing, not even the streaming of blood in his veins; he did not have the feeling either of being somewhere else, because he was nowhere, though, for the first time in his life, he was everywhere at the same time, at once present in everything. He recognized in everything that constituted his world his own child, himself, and he himself was the child of that child created by him.

His feverish brain seemed to have comprehended that his being the birthplace of the sense of time and of the conception of time was probably the decisive trait of his own nature; his conception of time was divided into a future and a past as well as a present; the latter, though real, was without boundaries and as such it stubbornly opposed the might of reason, of which the strange food, content and children were all sorts of limits and boundaries.

And because that elusive present flowed and did not know any rest, it could never be experienced directly, but always in retrospect, as the back of the divinity passing by quietly in the form of the deafening hustle and bustle on the world stage.

The birthplace of all of it was his brain, even of the idea of the inevitable development, thus also of the law of causality, hence of the idea that once there had been no world and that once again there will be no world, and eventually of the idea that there was something called matter, which played and gave birth to something called consciousness, the knowledge of oneself, of one's own ideas and of one's own knowledge, and thus invented and created itself and everything else.

The way out, towards all that constituted the so-called world, ended in the conscious being; the way into, towards the conscious being, ended in the world.

There was no doubt that these two tacks had to be trodden simultaneously, that only both of them together constituted that famous tube, called Cana, which is in Galilee, the land of waves and heaps of stones, that is of moving and resting, vanishing and persisting, in short: of form; and what was form if not that which had the ability to present itself as fleeting?

In Cana, inside the magnificent tube, a unification and amalgamation took place, the marriage, the wedding of the world, in which water as something neutral changed into the intoxicating wine of reality, filled with attraction and repulsion, joy and sorrow, sense and nonsense, desperation and hope.

What fault could be found with that train of thought, which showed completely that even the tiniest probability was the breeding ground of the indisputable reality, which, in turn, in the core of the brain as its ultimate stage of development – called consciousness by conscious creatures – had to be the mother of that tiniest probability?

Could thinking go any further at all? Did that thought not contain the thinking of thinking, for the child had given birth to the mother by whom it had been born?

The labyrinth was behind and the plain flooded by the light lay spread in front of the seeker who had looked for and found the exit.

The lurking bull-monster just before the final point, the power of the world experienced in a vulgar way, the last obstacle on the path to the state of the true human being, was overcome and the fatal, form-devouring sphinx deprived of its power.

Everything that had determined his previous life now appeared to Blasius like a strange, bad dream. It was an extremely laborious, painful way, however, obviously a necessary one.

Now he was standing on top of that mountain, the summit of which was – due to the nature of things – always above all the thick clouds and the only drawback of which was that from there it was absolutely impossible to tell those below the impenetrable cloud layer what it was like above it, unless a double germ of everything above the cloud was packed into a word that has the form of an unsinkable ship, of an ark, and sent out on a voyage on the never-ending floods of time in the hope that the ark would reach exactly that one who in silent solitude was sitting at the window, musing on *the* question in quest of a satisfactory answer, and looking forward to the redemptive word without bothering about the hour of its arrival.

*

One of the two windows in his room which had been open all the time, slammed shut all of a sudden as if flung by an invisible hand and shook him rudely out of his thoughts. Blasius turned around, startled, and for a while remained sitting and staring at the slammed window without stirring. He was trying to explain to himself the unexpected slamming of the window – the single still open window did not move. He stood up, walked toward the slammed window, opened it gingerly, examined with his thin finger tips the edges of both leaves of the casement and the lock, trying to conclude the cause from the consequences; then he looked out. Nothing particular could be noticed. He was quite surprised to see that there were no cracks in the window panes, although the slamming had been extraordinarily powerful; they were complete, undamaged and ready to continue to make the world inside and the world outside appear separate and united simultaneously.

"This is the second time that the window in my room has slammed shut inexplicably: there is no wind, it is as calm as it can be; it was probably a draught; an extremely weak one, and yet sufficient."

He was revolving such and similar thoughts in his mind, but he knew that there could be no draught, because the temperature of the air in his room and outside was the same, for those windows had been open all the time.

He inwardly dismissed all the speculations and expressed it spontaneously with a dismissive hand gesture.

"Oh, that is just ridiculous speculation," he said, barely audibly.

"Now two are shut, one is still open. I must hurry up and I must not waste even a second," he added.

He turned around, walked to his desk, sat down and began to write. He spoke aloud what he wrote, read, in fact, what he had already written down, as if to make sure not to have forgotten anything.

"The so-called matter creates man, and what calls itself man invents so-called matter and recognizes in its own invention its eternal mother, home and origin, its way and its destination in one.

That is the explanation of the greatest and, in fact, the only puzzle, for all other puzzles, mere fragments of the whole, are included in it. The wonderful aspect of this puzzle is that its solution makes it even more appealing."

Suddenly he laid down the pen, straightened up and looked into the void.

He remained in that position only for a few moments then suddenly bent over the desk, as if thunderstruck, and continued writing feverishly.

"I did not plan it, but obviously it was bound to happen. My insatiable desire for clarity in everything and justification for everything brought about that I wanted to create a mathematically clear, logical religion. That led me to the insight of which I otherwise could not have had even the slightest idea. It is the insight that robs me of everything I used to possess.

Now my previous possession is replaced by the insight itself, the knowledge of the state of affairs.

Now I am without consolation, without hope, without fear. All such things are concomitants of the religious ideas of God.

What I have attained now is the pure insight, and I know that I am not fooling myself into something, because it does not give anything but itself; it does not promise anything, and all it could promise comes along with it as a faithful, inseparable companion.

It abolishes the past and the future, converts them into the flowing present that never begins and never ends, because in it the beginning and the end are blended with each other.

It does not command that one has to love his God and must not seek any other. It instead makes one understand the meaning of the name Emanuel; thanks to it one realizes that the world-creating divinity is, in fact, the core of the essence of the human being.

It does not command that one should love his neighbour as himself, because thanks to it, each one recognizes himself in every other human being and therefore loves every other person without being ordered to do so.

Once this insight is attained, all the commandments and prohibitions turn out to be superfluous, because due to it everything happens as a matter of course, just for joy, not for fear of punishment or in anticipation of a reward.

Without this insight everything is but a heap of purposes; with it everything attains its deeper meaning.

Yes, yes, yes, this insight weighs more than all the commandments and prohibitions, regulations and laws of this world, upon which all sorts of religious and political systems are based."

Blasius sat down in his chair again and leaned far back; his arms hung down by the armrests. His face was directed towards the ceiling, his eyes were closed.

"Only now do I believe I understand the meaning of the idea that the world is not this way or that way, but that it corresponds exactly to human insight."

He leaned forward again over the desk and continued to write.

"The world is the child of the imbalance, that is, the preponderance of the forces which the Hebrews referred to when they spoke of the world-creating divinity.

The imbalance results from the preponderance of votes of the angels who support and encourage the creation, that is, of the acting possibilities. Thanks to that imbalance, each developing world order tips and topples in favour of the coming one. This tipping and toppling is what we call the course of the world, the essence of order in the midst of disorder, *tohuvabohu*, cosmos in chaos.

Even the slightest possibility that something happens is a double germ of the future world, which always suffices. This germ-couple is doubly fertile, because it builds up while destroying and destroys while building up. It is always in safe keeping in the belly of the word-ark, which is called Tewa, which floats on the stream of time and carries the decisive insight, the one which grants peace of mind.

The double germ, the fertile couple, consists of an acting possibility and of an imaginary one, of a one and a zero as it were.

The acting possibilities shape the world just as we experience it in each moment. At the same time they provoke us to speculate about the different forms and shapes the world could take on and what would be there if this world disappeared. The resulting images and ideas are based only on imaginary possibilities.

The imaginary possibilities are those disappointed angels who as permanent residents of human mind – according to the legend – are against the existence of man.

The double seed sprouts neither slowly nor fast. By bursting and sprouting it is newly formed. Its new formation is in turn both its bursting and its sprouting. It is that famous paradisiacal tree of life, which itself at the same time is a fruit and makes a fruit. Man should eat only fruit from that tree, because its essence is affirmation of the value of life. To eat something means to take in and assimilate and thus let it become the content of one's own self. We hardly ever think of this deep meaning of the word 'eat'.

The other paradisiacal tree is the life-hostile world view based on the chronological and spatial limits called beginning and end. According to the charming legend, man should not eat from that absurd and senseless world view, which is, of course, far less demanding and therefore prevailing.

For those who have understood the nature of the germ-couple, it is relevant only that the process of bursting and sprouting occurs, in short, that the world is there. The question when the world began and when it will end provides only stuff for entertainment and speculation for would-be scientists.

The appearance of man is the most improbable thing of all. It is the content of both the eternally active possibilities and the ones that are only thought, for man creates the supporting and the hindering angels, the same ones by whom he is created. The appearance of man is the event of all events, the actual source of the world, for all other events are contained in it.

Only now I believe I understand what man is and the meaning of those words in the temple that urge each individual to try to know the essence of one's own self. The taciturn sage who must have uttered them has said everything.

Only now I believe I understand the meaning of my own formulation of the theory of probabilities, the child of my mathematical endeavours to create a rational God: an external world creator is superfluous."

*

The birth of this idea delivered the death-blow to the former Blasius, the most ardent adherent of a religious movement, the advocate of the strictest religious formalism and the author of some brilliant polemical writings.

In these moments, he experienced at once the death of his former and the birth of his new self – he disappeared and emerged at the same time.

The process of creation out of vanishing occurred in him with such an incredible intensity that he had difficulty in writing down all his thoughts and feelings in a clear and orderly way. He felt that he was passing through the last moments of his fourth act, and what he was granted in those few moments made all his previous thoughts and insights appear completely meaningless.

He knew he had won everything, without having to bet or throw the dice for the favour of some fictitious God.

The bet he once emphatically demanded now appeared to him to be nothing less than the most abominable blasphemy, which he had uttered in a state of ignorance and fundamental misunderstanding of the world.

With frantic movements and strongly trembling hands, he hastily wrote the last lines, which the interplay of forces yet granted to him.

The lines ran diagonally, crossed one another; most of the letters were badly distorted, many words barely legible, for he saw nothing more.

What he now wrote, was his will, the plea to his sister to accept his new birth.

"Dearest Berti," he wrote, "please be so kind and remove the sheet from the lining of my coat and destroy it. I wrote something on it while I was still dead.

See to it that what you can read on these sheets on the desk gets known. This is the child of my resurrection, and also that which is still lacking in the spiral of human insight and therefore in the birth of man, its final turn, the free end of which leads back to the starting point, the eye. From there you can see the whole development and also know exactly where you are. Seen from there, no further development is disturbing, because it is always in the centre, always contained in the eye."

A scream escaped his mouth, and he scribbled down ever larger and more indistinct letters, passing into a wavy line, and a long-stretched arc ending in a large ink stain intended to be the point of the exclamation mark after the last word.

"Do that in my memory!"

The pen fell from his lifeless hand, and his body slumped into the armchair.

The candle flickered, consuming the last drop of wax, and went out. The written-on sheets came within a whisker of catching fire, however the tiny element that was lacking had decided against it.

***

Since her brother moved to live with her, Gilberte had much more work to do, because Blasius was gravely ill, fanatical and fastidious. She experienced the unpleasant consequences of all that every day – she was exhausted and needed nothing so much as a good sleep.

After the visitors of Port-Royal, whom Blasius did not want to receive had left, she retired to her room and went straight to bed, yet she could not get to sleep, because the constant whispers and murmurs which came no doubt from Blasius' room kept her awake.

However, that alone was not the main reason. It was rather the completely incomprehensible behaviour of her brother towards the people of Port-Royal, whom he used to support by every means and with the utmost readiness, which wouldn't allow her to sleep.

It was obvious that in him something strange must have happened, and she tried to find an explanation for that. She rejected everything that came to her mind as absurd and impossible and didn't consider it any further.

The disturbed, deadly serious expression of her brother and the unfriendly and harsh tone in which he had ordered her to send away people who, until only a day before, used to be his most welcome visitors, had shocked her.

*

As soon as she had heard the scream, she ran into his room, for she had a bad foreboding.

There was no light in Blasius' room.

The small three-armed candlestick high up in her hand, she walked slowly and almost noiselessly towards his desk.

The sight that presented itself to her in the flickering candlelight was frightening. Her brother's body, which had always been thin and slender, was now collapsed into a paltry lump and looked even smaller and more miserable than only a few hours before. His haggard face was disfigured with pain and betrayed the intensity of the final struggle that he had prolonged, by his iron will, to wring a few moments of the most precious earthly treasure from the angel of death and to write down at any price the insight he had just got. He did it in order to be retained in the memory of future generations not as someone who – although a good mathematician –was yet a poor half-wit, but as somebody who could offer satisfactory answers to the crucial questions concerning human existence to all alert people whose main concern was peace of mind.

She managed to overcome the strange barrier that separated her from the lump in the armchair. She turned to that something in front of her with an unaffected and unstudied sincerity, although she felt that no one could reply.

"Brother!" she said briskly, "I heard you scream, what happened?"

She knew that she was insane, because she was aware that she was talking to a corpse that could not answer any more than a lump of ice or a gravel pile. She knew that all that could happen had happened to that one whose mortal coil was lying in the armchair in front of her.

"My God! Brother, dear soul!"

She tried to wake him, called him again, then a third time, although she knew that she shouted into the void. She did it despite that knowledge in order to scare away the doubting angels of pure reasoning and because the dead suck the navels of the living, urging them to think ceaselessly of those who are gone for good and all. The former stop thinking of the dead in the moment of their own decease, that is, only when they join them. Then they turn round, like a sand-glass, and start sucking the navels of the living, visit them in their thoughts and dreams, convert the past into the future.

She put the candle carefully on the desk, sat down on the soft, round arm of the chair and gently lifted the eyelids which once belonged to her brother and which sometimes used to open in a wild manner, making his melancholy black eyes light up. It was the gaze that she both loved and almost feared.

All she met now was rigid, dead indifference.

"He is gone," escaped her lips.

*

The quill-pen was lying on the freshly written-on sheets; the ink was still wet. The crooked and irregular lines and the long, wavy final line with the big ink stain aroused her curiosity.

She took the top sheet on the desk and began reading. She read slowly aloud, although no one was listening to her, except the invisible listener, who is always and everywhere present where the human imagination lives.

It took a while before she managed to decipher all that Blasius had written in the last hours of his painful life, because the writing was hardly legible. Gilberte knew her brother's writing and she found her way where an outsider would have had to give up.

When she had read the last lines in which he asked her to remove the sewn-in sheet from his coat and destroy it, then to see to it that his last thoughts be published, for mankind was lacking exactly that insight which he had struggled through, she dropped her hand on her lap and gave the dead body in the chair a quick, cursory glance which contained besides grief also a dose of compassion.

"My poor brother," she said, barely audibly, "turned insane before his death. God in his wisdom and mercy has freed him from his torment."

She laid the sheet on the desk and sat down in the chair next to it.

"All he has recently written," she whispered, "must be worthless, because he looked bewildered."

She picked up all the notes, some of which were lying on the desk and some on the floor, and tore them into small pieces.

"It is good that nobody except me is awake now. I am undisturbed and can think calmly about what to do, so that of all the things my poor brother has written, only those that make sense become known for posterity.

But first I must find out what's on the sewn-in sheet. So that was the reason why the coat wasn't supposed to be washed or cleaned."

*

It was not easy to divest the dead body of the coat, but she finally managed it somehow. She tore at the lining of the jacket and took out the sewn-in sheet. Then she read what was on it, muttering.

"This is exactly the way he thought when he was still entirely sane despite his general physical weakness; this is what he wrote in the moments of his highest spiritual flights," she thought, "in the moments when God directly spoke to him. The present world and the future should learn about these lines," she spoke resolutely, "and not of that nonsense he scribbled in complete mental derangement in the last minutes of his life. I will sew the sheet back in and then ask Louise to unpick all of his clothes and search carefully. It is better that it be found in his coat than on his desk. Then there can be no doubt that the content of the text on the sheet was something that he appreciated more than anything else in his life, his legacy."

She carefully picked up even the smallest scraps of paper so that there would be no traces of the last moments of his life either on the desk or on the floor. Then she pressed the scraps between her clenched fingers and was about to leave the room.

"It is good that there is still a fire burning in the fireplace downstairs," she murmured, acting rather hastily as if afraid someone might suddenly appear and prevent her from carrying out what she intended to do.

She quickly went to the one still open window intending to shut it. Then, however, she turned and glanced at the dead lump in the chair and let the side of the window gently go out of her hand.

Before she left the room, she looked around again, as if making sure that the fourth act was definitely over and the stage ready for the next, the decisive one.

Then she stepped into the hallway and shut the door behind her.

The streaming blood in her veins and the blazing flames in the fireplace did not allow her to hear the creaking steps under her feet as she was hurrying downstairs.

Choirs of otherwise inaudible voices that emanate from all things, especially the silent ones, thanked the main hero for his manifested resoluteness to persevere and his readiness to give in, with an applause audible only for those who dream in their waking hours.

One of the windows in Blasius' room remained open.

*****

www.ingramcontent.com/pod-product-compliance
Lightning Source LLC
Chambersburg PA
CBHW030809310726
48980CB00006B/430/J
* 9 7 8 3 9 5 2 3 8 5 9 4 4 *